Redwood High

As soon as Celia pulled herself onto the tree house floor, they all got comfortable — Sean's legs under the bridge of Allie's knees, Celia with her back against Allie's shoulder, Meg's ankle over the crook of Nick's arm.

A warm, dry wind blew over them, typical of a Northern California September. Birds squalled. Hughie barked. Overhead the leaves rustled.

"High school. . . ." Celia sighed dreamily.

"Homework . . ." Nick teased, poking his cousin.

They all laughed, and Allie poked Celia, too. Still, there was no joke that could dampen the excitement they felt about tomorrow, their first day at brand-new Redwood High.

CLASS of '88

by Linda A. Cooney

Freshman
Sophomore
Junior
Senior

CLASS of '88

FRESHMAN

Linda A. Cooney

SCHOLASTIC INC.
New York Toronto London Auckland Sydney

ISBN 0-590-40348-6

12 11 10 9 8 7 6 5 4 3 2 1   7 8 9/8 0 1 2/9

Printed in the U.S.A.   01

First Scholastic printing, June 1987

CHAPTER 1

Fourteen-year-old Meg McCall balanced her foot on the roof of the old doghouse, stretched to grab the branch overhead, and began to climb. Bark scratched her palms but she barely felt it. Leaves swept her face and caught in her long hair, but she didn't care.

"C'mon, everybody!" she yelled.

She hoped they were all behind her — Nick and his cousin Celia, Allie, and Sean. They were Meg's best and oldest friends in the entire world.

The trunk shook and the branches rattled as Meg pulled herself up and scooted across the tree house floor. Sean's head popped up next, two twigs stuck in his red hair. He drummed the wooden floor and grinned.

"I'm here. Let's rock 'n' roll," he said.

But Allie and Celia were still below, whispering and giggling. Meg cupped her hands and yelled, "Hurry up, you guys!"

1

Allie and Celia looked at one another, then climbed up together. They did everything together, even though they looked very different. Celia was willowy and blonde, almost beautiful in a flea market dress and white sun hat, whereas Allie was small and roundish and her clothes were wild. Today Allie wore jangly plastic bracelets, purple shorts, a pink blouse, and Gumby barrettes in her wispy brown hair. As she climbed into the tree house, her bracelets clattered and clacked.

"Where's Nick?" Meg worried. They couldn't do anything without Nick. He and Meg were the group's unofficial leaders.

Sean scrunched up his freckled face. "I thought he got up here first."

"Me, too," Allie and Celia said at the same time.

Meg looked back down over the edge. No one — just Hughie's doghouse against the deep green of the lawn, the swimming pool, the apple orchard, and Nick's house. But when the branches above separated and leaves fluttered down, Meg broke into a huge smile.

"Nick Rhodes, you turkey," Meg taunted, tipping her face to the sky.

"Surprise." Nick laughed and stuck his head down between the patchy leaves. He had climbed almost to the top, and his muscular, lean body was stretched out over the tree. Before Meg could warn him to be careful, he spread his arms and leaped.

"Ahhahhahh!" he yodeled like Tarzan as he dropped, falling on Meg and pulling her down to the rough planked floor.

2

"Nick!" she shrieked, but he tickled her any-way. She gasped and giggled, feeling the floor shake and wobble beneath her. "You're crazy."

"Oh, yeah?" His green eyes sparkled, but when he reached out to grab Meg again, she fought him off. Finally, both of them sat back, panting and smiling.

It was quiet as the five of them got comfortable — Sean's legs under the bridge of Allie's knees; Celia's back against Allie's shoulder; Meg's ankle over the crook of Nick's arm. A warm, dry wind blew over them, typical of a Northern California September. Birds squalled. Hughie barked. Over-head the leaves crackled and swayed.

"High school. . . ." Celia sighed dreamily.

"Homework . . ." Nick teased, poking his cousin.

They all laughed, and Allie poked Celia, too. Still, there was no joke that could dampen the excitement they felt about tomorrow, their first day as freshmen at brand-new Redwood High. Pretty soon they were all talking at once.

"I heard Redwood has this room with thirty Apple computers," Sean said.

Celia leaned in. "Everyone says it's all super modern. I'm so glad they closed old Sonoma High. Was that ever gross."

"You know they left some old farm house on the Redwood campus," Allie marveled, "from when it was still Miller's ranch. My dad drove me by the other day and you can see the farm house from the street. It looks so weird next to all the new stuff."

"I heard the football stadium doesn't have any

lights yet, but we're going to play in the league anyway," added Nick.

"All those upperclassmen from Sonoma. And I heard our class will be from three different middle schools." Celia's eyes were wide with excitement. "And Oakwood Private, too."

Allie giggled at the mention of Oakwood Private and pushed up the tip of her nose. Celia playfully slapped her. "I know those girls are snobs, but think of all the new people. I've been waiting for this for fourteen years. Real dances — where people actually dance instead of standing around like geeks. Real football games — "

"Real boys," Allie interrupted, "and maybe my parents will finally believe I'm not five years old anymore."

Suddenly they all looked to Meg again. She knew they'd noticed the serious expression on her face, but she couldn't help it. Nick lightly touched her arm. "Aren't you excited, Meg?" His voice was soft, sweet. For a second, he was the boy Meg had traded bug cages with and not the handsome freshman about to enter Redwood High.

Meg pulled at a nail in the floor. What was wrong with her? She'd been as excited as the rest of them about Redwood; in fact, she'd been talking about it nonstop since last June. Still, she had this funny feeling inside. In spite of everything — the classes, the new campus, the different people they'd meet — Meg felt a vague sadness. It wasn't as if she had a bad sunburn or a terrible charley horse, only this tiny ache in her heart.

But her friends were waiting for her to say something. She was Meg the leader, after all, one of the best students, and president of the eighth-grade class. Allie and Celia said she was pretty, too, with eyes the color of Nick's swimming pool and waist-length dark hair. Her friends had no doubts that for Meg McCall, Redwood would be great.

"Sure, I'm excited about Redwood High," Meg said slowly, trying to put a finger on what hurt. "I think maybe it's the tree house."

"The tree house." Celia sighed. "I thought we'd all finally decided."

They *had* decided, Meg realized. This was to be the final visit to the tree house. Celia said tree houses were only for little kids. Of course, Allie had agreed — she and Celia agreed on most everything. Nick said he didn't care, and Sean said the only time he wanted to go up was to watch comets. Even Meg had to admit that the tree house was getting pretty crowded when all of them sat in it together. Still, she didn't want to let it go. There were so many important things here: Allie's fashion drawings tacked to a branch, Meg's seventh-grade track trophy on a shelf next to Celia's thrift store knickknacks, the old tube radio that Sean had lovingly restored to life.

Meg's seriousness finally rubbed off on the others. Celia shifted uneasily. Sean began whistling under his breath, and Nick picked gravel out of his tennis shoe. Finally Allie lifted a hand and her plastic bracelets clattered for attention. "I know. We should do a good-bye ceremony or something!"

"Like when we tried to be blood brothers and sisters when we were ten?"

Celia ruffled Sean's hair. "Don't be gross."

Meg sat up, the energy returning to her long limbs. Allie was right. They should have a ceremony, something to make sure that even though they were going to high school, they still remained the closest people in the world.

"Yes! Let's tell a secret!" Meg decided. They all sat up. "Something that you've never told anybody, that nobody else outside of us can ever know."

"Yeah!"

"A secret."

"Let me think."

Again they settled into silence. The sunlight flickered along the wooden floor, and the branches continued to wave and rustle overhead.

Sean was the first to lean forward. He slipped his bare, freckled legs out from under Allie's knees and huddled close to the center of the circle. "Okay," he said, "I'm ready."

The others applauded, and Meg decided that this was a really good idea. She held on to the tree trunk behind her and focused on Sean.

"Remember the fire in my backyard?"

Nick nodded. "The one the lightning started."

"Yeah," agreed Celia. "I'll never forget my mom running out when your palm tree went up right across from our fence."

Sean made a face. "She had that weird green stuff on her face. . . ."

"A mud mask. For her complexion," Celia informed.

"Whatever," shrugged Sean. "I thought it meant she'd already been burned up."

They laughed, remembering how the quick reactions of Sean's neighbors — mainly Meg's parents and Celia's mom — saved Sean's house from disaster.

"So what's the secret?" Nick asked.

"Well. . . ." Sean shifted his narrow shoulders. "You know those rockets I was into?" He paused and swallowed, trying to keep his voice on an even plane. Lately his voice had started to slide from high to low like a derailed roller coaster. "The ones my dad told me I couldn't shoot off anymore. . . ."

Celia's mouth fell open. "You mean *you* started that fire? Sean, you almost burned down my house, too!"

Sean looked a little worried. "You won't tell, will you?"

Heads turned while five pairs of eyes made contact. Nothing needed to be said. Of course no one would tell.

"I'll go next," volunteered Celia.

Celia sat up as Sean relaxed. Her blonde hair floated to her shoulders, almost the same color as her pale yellow sundress. But her eyes, which sometimes looked blue, sometimes sea green, were now guarded and cloudy. "You can't tell this. I've never told anybody, not even Allie."

She looked up to make sure that her command was well taken. It was.

"Okay. In seventh grade I stole a pair of earrings from Macy's in San Francisco. I really wanted these dumb earrings, like some of the other girls had, and my mom wouldn't buy them for me because it was right after the divorce, and she was really paranoid about money." Celia's eyes went back to the floor. "So when Mom wasn't looking, I put them in my pocket." Celia raised her head. "Afterward I felt so awful, I buried the earrings in the backyard." She frowned. "I wonder if they're still there."

"Oh, Cici," Allie sympathized. She touched Celia's hand and Celia shrugged.

Celia turned to her cousin Nick and tapped his shin. "Your turn."

Nick was still crouching, holding on to the trunk behind him. He stared up between the leaves and squinted. "I guess the worst secret I have is about my last year of Little League. We were in the playoffs, and my dad was all excited about us winning, 'cause both my brothers' teams had won before us. Then right at the end of the game I made this brutal error. I just dropped the ball like a total jerk. There was no reason for it — I just fumbled it — but I pretended like my arm was hurt all of a sudden. They took me out of the game. Afterward my parents sent me to two different doctors — "

Meg interrupted. "I always wondered about that."

Nick smiled at her. "It figures you'd see through it."

"Wait," demanded Celia. "You were never really hurt at all?"

Nick looked away. "It was all a fake."

They all shook their heads. It was amazing . . . strong, straightforward Nick pulling a stunt like that. Of course, Celia's and Sean's confessions were just as amazing. But as the lull continued,

Meg knew that this pact was a good idea. They were creating a bond and nothing would ever break it.

"I guess it's my turn," said Allie, brushing away a lock of wispy brown curls. "But I don't think I can tell mine in front of boys."

"Oh, come on," urged Sean. "We're not like ordinary boys, we're more like brothers."

Allie, who had a younger brother, rolled her eyes. "That's even worse."

"We told ours," demanded Celia. "Now you. It's only fair."

"Okay." Allie chewed on her thumbnail. "You know that swim party you had in the spring, Nick?"

"Sure."

Allie suddenly started to giggle and blush. Her hand went to her face. "This is so embarrassing!"

"Come on."

But Allie just laughed harder with her bouncy, infectious giggle. When Allie went off on her laughing jags, the others always went, too. Allie flapped her small hands to try and gain control. "It was my first coed swim party — my parents made this big deal out of it, you know, was I old enough — like it was some big deal to go swimming around boys. So I wanted everyone to think I was really cool" — she started to laugh so hard she was wheezing — "so I wore a bra under my bathing suit. . . ."

Sean looked puzzled. "What's so weird about that?"

They all laughed harder.

Under his freckles, Sean was turning the color

of ripe watermelon. "You mean, girls don't wear bras under their bathing suits?" On the word "bras" his voice cracked, but Nick threw an affectionate arm around him, taking the shame away. Now Sean was laughing, too. The tree was starting to shake.

Allie, still laughing and holding her stomach, wiped away a tear. "Anyway, it wasn't until I got out of the water, and there was this strap falling down my arm, that I realized that none of the other girls were wearing bras under their bathing suits. . . ."

"So what did you do?"

"I didn't even tell Cici, I just ran home, went to my room, and hid for the rest of the party. I was so embarrassed." Allie put a hand to her chest. "And don't any of you dare tell anybody!"

"Don't worry," gulped Sean.

The helpless giggling ceased, but as Meg's turn approached, she found it hard to talk. She no longer felt so worried about the tree house, but she was overwhelmed by something else. It was a feeling brought on by Allie's goofy intensity, Celia's grace and beauty, Sean's unique smarts and sweetness, and Nick's sturdiness, daring, and warmth. Lately Nick just looked at her and she got that feeling. She found herself staring at the clean line of his jaw and the muscular curve of his shoulder. Meg couldn't help thinking back to the hundreds of foot races she and Nick had run, the books they had read together, the adventures they had shared. How they had tickled, hollered, collected, hid, invented, confessed, and joked.

"Meg, it's your turn," Nick was saying.

Rising to her knees, Meg looked at her four friends and drew a long breath. They all were waiting for her, but no deep, dark secret would come to mind. Of course, there were awful times when she'd lied or chickened out or messed up, but she'd shared those humiliations with her friends already. Her mind could bring up only one theme.

"Maybe it's not some terrible secret," Meg said at last, "but it's the total truth, and it's something that I'd never ever say to any other four friends."

"What?" asked Nick.

Meg was hit with a sudden wave of shyness and looked down. "Just that I love you all. And I will forever."

Allie's eyes watered. Celia bit her lip. Sean blushed. Nick nodded.

Nobody said a word.

CHAPTER 2

"Celia, honey, if you want me to drive you to school, hurry up!"

"Mom, I'm almost ready."

"You've been in there forever."

Celia couldn't work any faster. Every time she tried, the mascara tube flew out of her fingers and rolled behind the toilet, or her curling iron slipped and produced a lump of blonde frizz. Her hands were shaking with excitement, and she'd been awake since five, selecting and reselecting the perfect first-day-of-school outfit. Her talent for finding designer look-alikes at thrift stores and flea markets was impressive at Portola Middle School, but this was high school. There would be upperclassmen, rich girls from Oakwood Private.

She wondered if she could call Allie. But Allie was probably already driving in with Nick — they lived on the other side of Redwood High. Meg had gone in early to sign up for Honors English.

Sean had ridden his bike. They were meeting in the parking lot as soon as they all arrived . . . and at lunch . . . and every chance they could get after that.

The bathroom door opened a crack. Mrs. Cavanaugh leaned in.

"Cici, let's go." Then the door swung all the way open. Celia got a good look at her mom and nearly dropped her mascara.

"Mom, what did you do?"

"What?"

"Your hair!"

Celia cringed. Her mom, who was a hairdresser at a salon in downtown Redwood Hills, had put a streak in her hair that was somewhere between blue and lavender.

"Mom, that looks sick."

Her mom touched her short blonde hair and laughed. "It's a new tint I wanted to try. Cici, if you want me to drive you, let's hit it."

Celia stared at her mother and felt panic starting to swell inside her. This was crazy. She wasn't supposed to be telling her mother how to look. But it happened a lot — like that party last summer for Nick's dad. He was a California state senator, so there'd been a ton of important people, plus Meg's folks and Sean's and Allie's. So what did her mother do the day before? All Celia knew was that it had ended up looking like something between electric shock treatment and Bozo the Clown.

"Mom, you've got to change that."

Her mother laughed as she looked for her keys. "It's a little late now, Cici. Let's go."

"But, Mom. . . ."

It was too late, her mother was gone — out the front door and heading for the car. Celia felt a rush of panic. She tried to hold it inside as she grabbed her purse and her notebook. But when she opened the front door and saw the rusty old Datsun puffing blue exhaust, she couldn't take it. The thought of her mom being seen by the other freshmen, by sophomores and seniors, by girls from Oakwood Private. . . . No way. Celia marched up to her mother's window.

"Mom."

Mrs. Cavanaugh reached across the front seat and opened the passenger door. "Cici, get in."

"Mom, I'm going to walk," Celia blurted. Then she looked away.

"What?"

Celia made the words come out but kept her eyes straight to the ground. "No, really. I'd rather walk. I have time."

The car rumbled, then choked, and finally stopped. Her mother pushed back the seatbelt and threw open the door. "Fine," she said as Celia turned away from her. "Start walking."

Allie's heart was not beating fast. Her stomach didn't clench, her bracelets weren't jangling, and her palms were perfectly dry. In fact, she wasn't at all nervous, but if her father kept telling her not to be scared, and if they didn't get to school soon, she just might lose it.

"Don't be nervous, Allie," Mr. Simon said for the fourteenth time.

"I'm not, Dad."

"You know how you are."

No! Allie felt like yelling, I know how *you* are. Since the birth of Allie's sister four months ago, Mr. Simon had taken full charge of Allie. It was embarrassing enough for them to have a baby at their age, and now her mom was busy all the time at home, and her father was driving her totally crazy. "It's okay, Dad. I feel fine."

"How about you, Nick?"

Nick, who sat confidently in the backseat, smiled. "I'm great."

Mr. Simon carefully changed lanes. Finally he held up a hand. "There it is," he announced.

Nick and Allie both gasped. Now Allie really did feel butterflies. There it was, the new school. Big redwoods everywhere. Classrooms clumped in twos and threes surrounded by impossibly perfect green grass. The only things that didn't look brand-new were the big trees and the old farm house left over from when it was Miller's ranch.

"It sure doesn't look like a school," Allie breathed.

"Yeah," Nick agreed. "More like a country club. I told my dad that, and all he could say was that I better not act like it's a country club."

The laughter broke the tension, and Allie felt a little bit of relief, but she could also see from her father's face in the mirror that he was becoming more anxious. "I'm not so sure about the parking situation," Mr. Simon worried. "Allie, now you be careful when I let you out."

Finally they pulled into the main entrance. Before them stood the flagpole and behind that the main offices and the woodsy campus. A red and blue "Welcome Grizzlies" banner hung between two tall trees. As Mr. Simon parked, Celia, Meg, and Sean walked out of the main building and spotted them. Meg jumped up and down, Celia waved, and Sean whistled loudly.

"Thanks, Mr. Simon," Nick said cheerfully, as he made faces back at them through the window. He pushed on the door handle, but when it didn't open, he looked confused.

"Dad. . . ." Allie reminded.

"Just be careful," her father said for about the umpteenth time. Then he reached for the button that unlocked all the doors.

"Thanks," Nick called as he scooted out.

" 'Bye, Dad. Thanks for taking us."

"Allie, I'll pick you up. Be waiting by the flagpole. Don't wander off."

"Okay, Dad."

"I know how you like to wander off by yourself. Be care — "

Before her father could tell her to be careful about anything else, Allie bolted out the door and joined her friends.

For Meg, the whole first morning was a wonderful blur.

Her teachers were pretty interesting, especially Mr. Hallmark, her history teacher, who told them all that since it was a new school they were going to have to take their shoes off every time they came into his room. The classrooms were so clean and bright, all with huge windows and surrounding the woodsy quad, it almost looked like Capitola Park. The lockers were all painted green and royal blue, and the hallways were a mixture of emotional reunions, first-day fashion shows, and a rush of kids who looked much older, bigger, and more confident than she did. But the best part she had to wait for: lunchtime! The chance, at last, to hear how everybody was doing since the first bell rang. Meg couldn't help smiling as she plunged ahead.

But once inside, Meg realized that the Redwood cafeteria was *huge*. Besides the regular cafeteria line, there was a deli counter, a salad bar, and something called The Soup Stop. The place was so new it still smelled more of floor wax than of ravioli. And there were so many tables! Meg stood in the doorway, temporarily paralyzed, not sure which table she should take.

Still she had to find a place. At Portola Middle School she and her friends had always had the same table. It was known as the McCall-Rhodes Bar and Grill, after her and Nick, and it sat right in the middle of the cafeteria. It was the place that everybody stopped at to find out what was up in the student council, how the prom was coming, or just to tell jokes or share food or say hello. Meg couldn't imagine eating lunch without that kind of home base. So she finally rushed in and blindly put her books down on the first empty table she could find, then turned around to look for Nick. She didn't see him, but from her right she heard a yell.

"MEG!!!"

It was Celia and Allie. They were on the other side of a group of sophomore boys. Celia was aggressively pushing her way through, but Allie was too shy and looked like she might get swept out into the hall, until Celia reached back and pulled her along.

"I saved us a table," Meg announced as the girls joined her.

"Thanks," Allie bubbled. She pulled up her bright blue culottes to sit cross-legged in the chair and took out a pink paper sack her mom had packed for her.

"How's it going?" Meg asked.

"We're still alive," they said at the same time.

"You should see the painting studio behind my art room," Allie glowed. "It has a skylight and everything."

"And my math teacher is totally gorgeous. He may actually get me to do my homework this year." Celia grinned, then looked at the cafeteria line and made a face. "That is a killer line. Al, can I have some of yours?"

Allie was already dividing her sandwich and cookies. "Sure."

Even though Meg was starving she couldn't think about food until she'd found Nick. Then Allie bobbed up, pointing to Sean as he came in. He was carrying a huge load of books with his bike helmet and lunch sack balanced on top.

"Boy, am I glad to see you guys," he said, after he had worked his way through the crowd. "So far today I've gotten lost and had two teachers mispronounce my name. Plus I think they gave me the wrong locker combination. But I found out they have all these cool science classes I can take in a year or two. Horticulture, astronomy, farm science. . . ."

Celia took his chips out of his paper sack and opened them. "Farm science . . ." she teased. "Who wants to take farm science?"

Sean laughed and plucked back his chips. "I don't know, but I still think it's cool that they teach it."

Meg grinned at her three friends. Celia looked so beautiful in her fluffy white sweater and yellow skirt that it was impossible to see how every guy at Redwood wouldn't be after her. Allie had a let-me-take-all-this-in look in her eyes that was as wild as her Day-Glo socks and glittery barrettes. Sean, with his huge stack of books, looked like brain of the year . . . but where was Nick? For some reason Meg wanted Nick at this table most of all.

"HEY, YOU GUYS!"

Nick had burst into the cafeteria. There was no other way to describe it. There was a huge grin on his face, and the wave he gave them all was big enough to paint a barn. He was in a red polo shirt and brand-new jeans, and he seemed to stand out even in the busy crowd. Meg was so happy to see him, she bumped against the table and almost knocked over a chair when she jumped up to wave.

He hurried over, stopping to say hello to people and pat guys he knew from middle school on the back. Meg noticed more than a few girls put their sandwiches down to stare.

"Hi!" he breathed to Meg as he sat down. "Got this place scoped out."

"Yeah, what does that mean?" Meg giggled.

"You memorized the combination to your PE locker?"

"Cute." Nick smiled and bumped her with his elbow. "Much better than that." He flicked his hair away from his eyes and whipped open his notebook to read some notes clipped right inside. Meg leaned in to read over his shoulder.

"Okay. First off, there's no freshman football for this first year. . . ."

"Too bad," Sean came back. "I was going to try out for quarterback."

Nick laughed. "I ran into Coach Turner and he told me to think about Varsity. I guess since the school's new and all, he's going to be really open to freshmen. Same thing with cheerleading. For this year there's just going to be one squad, and they want freshmen to try out." He looked up at Celia. "They're going to explain it all at that orientation thing this afternoon."

Allie and Celia immediately grabbed each other's hands. "Let's try out!" they said at the same time.

Nick looked over at the caf line and stuck a hand in his jeans pocket to pull out some change. As he did Meg handed him an apple from her sack. He grabbed it, took a bite, and continued talking. "Did you all hear that announcement second period?"

"Which one?" laughed Celia. "It was great. The principal made so many announcements we almost didn't do anything in Balfour's Spanish class."

Allie nodded. "We were hoping it'd be like that every day."

"No such luck," Nick said. "I'm talking about the announcement he made about class presidents. You know, about submitting nominations?"

Meg put her head down, unable to meet the force of Nick's bright eyes. The principal had asked them to submit nominations for freshman officers so that they could have an election at the orientation meeting that afternoon. All the classes were having instant elections — no campaigns or speeches. Meg had thought about nominating Nick, but she knew he wanted to try out for football.

"Well," said Nick, "did anybody think of someone to nominate?"

"Nope."

"Nah."

Celia laughed. "If that dorky Martin Corfman gets it, I'll die."

Nick grinned. "Don't worry. He won't."

"How do you know?"

Nick smiled and then tugged on Meg's braid. Meg poked his middle, and Nick grabbed her wrist and started whistling a little tune as if he were taking a walk in the park.

"Come on, Rhodes," Meg teased. "Quit acting like a jerk and tell us what you know."

"Dum-de-dum-dum," Nick hummed in Meg's ear till Celia reached over and playfully slapped him on the head. "All right, all right," he said. "No more torture. I'll tell you."

"What?"

"There's another person nominated who's going to get it for sure."

Meg finally looked up. She was sitting very

close to him. "Yeah, how do you know that?"

" 'Cause I nominated her."

"And who is it?" Meg challenged.

"It's you, McCall."

"Me?"

"You."

Meg stared blankly. She didn't know why she was so shocked. After all, she was head of her class in middle school. Still, in the middle of this unfamiliar cafeteria, surrounded by strange tables, strange smells, and strange upperclassmen, the idea of taking charge of anything made her knees wobbly. She sunk back into her chair, and Nick sunk down next to her.

"Don't you want to run, Meg?" Nick asked sweetly. "I could withdraw your name if you really want me to."

Now they were all staring at her, as intently as they had the day before in the tree house.

Celia leaned in. "You'd do a great job, Meg."

"You will," Allie agreed.

Sean smiled. "I'll bet on it."

Nick leaned over and touched Meg's hand. "I thought you'd want to be nominated." He stared at her until she had to look away.

Meg took a deep breath. With Nick and the rest of her friends supporting her, anything seemed possible.

"Okay. I'll run," she managed.

Even over the din of the cafeteria Meg could hear them all cheer.

CHAPTER 3

"Believe me, I'm just as excited as the rest of you, but could you all take your seats so we can start this orientation."

The voice of Miss Meyer, the short, dark-haired freshman adviser, boomed across the length of the new auditorium. She stood on a shiny stage, backed by dark red curtains and a huge portrait of California conservationist John Muir.

Meg hugged her notebook against her chest, breathed in the smell of freshly laid carpet, and slowly sat down. Nick was next to her. Celia was on her other side. Sean and Allie were beside Celia. All of them still wanted her to run for president and were chattering away about it. She'd warned Nick that she probably couldn't win. Portola was the biggest middle school feeding into Redwood, but half the freshmen had no idea who she was — kids from Capitola Middle School, Sonoma Junior High, and Oakwood Private.

Meg held tight and listened as Miss Meyer explained over loud screeches of feedback how things were going to be a little unusual this first year. The newness of the school would give the freshmen extra opportunities and responsibilities. Redwood was not quite finished, and it would be up to each class to raise money to help complete the tennis courts, the senior garden, and the football stadium. Nick sat up as Miss Meyer described the need for stadium lights . . . which made Meg sit up, too.

"The Elks club and the Rotary have offered to help raise money for the lights," Miss Meyer announced. "But it's largely up to you, the freshmen. No lights, no night football games."

The whole class moaned, and Nick shook his head and smacked his fist against the arm of the chair. "What a drag," he whispered angrily. Another grumble traveled from their row all the way forward.

"So," Miss Meyer continued, an amazingly powerful voice coming out of her tiny body, "the first thing your new president will need to do is put together a fundraising committee and plan an event. The freshman fundraiser day is set for Friday, October twenty-sixth." Someone yelled out that it would be almost Halloween, and Miss Meyer held up her hands to stop the ghostly oooh's and ahhhh's. "You haven't much time."

Meg wanted to jump out of her seat. A fundraiser! That was the kind of thing she did so well.

Miss Meyer put on a pair of glasses and pulled a paper out of her jacket pocket. "I'd like to introduce your presidential candidates and hand out ballots so that we can have a winner by the end of orientation."

The crowd grew quiet as Miss Meyer read the nominations. When Meg's name was called, she stood up and took a teeny bow, then folded back into her seat. She squirmed to check out her opponents but recognized only Martin Corfman, the other candidate from Portola. Finally, pink mimeographed ballots were passed down the aisles and into the rows. As the paper landed in Meg's lap and she passed the stack on, Nick gave her wrist a squeeze. It was achingly quiet as the freshman class paused to scratch their X's and pass the ballots back.

When voting was finished, two teachers, Mr. Greer and Mrs. Wheeldon, collected the ballots and began to count them in the back as Miss Meyer went on to other business. Meg tried to keep her attention on the stage, but kept turning around, as if she could tell by the look on the teachers' faces who was going to win.

Miss Meyer held a clipboard and began to read announcements. "Let's see. Keep checking the bulletin board outside the main office for upcoming events, clubs, and auditions for band and pep squad. The first dance will be in four weeks."

Allie giggled. "A dance! Let's all go together."

Sean shushed her.

"Football and cross-country tryouts are posted in the gym. And don't forget the cheerleading tryouts. Mrs. Wong is going to talk to you about that. Mrs. Wong. . . ."

The entire group stirred. Talk broke out through the crowd. Mrs. Wong, an athletic-looking Asian woman with small glasses, blew into the microphone. "Hi," she said a little nervously.

"HI," the crowd roared back.

Everyone laughed.

Mrs. Wong held up one hand. "Okay. Since we're new and won't be having freshman teams. . . ."

This time there was a groan followed by some boos and hisses. The teacher took it good-naturedly and held up a finger. "It's not my fault. . . ."

More laughs.

"However, it's not all bad. Freshmen can try out for Junior Varsity and Varsity teams, and we're going to make an effort to include you. The same thing goes for cheerleading. Since there's so little time before the first game, we're only going to have one squad. But we're going to make sure that at least one girl from every class is on it. So don't hesitate to try out just because you're freshmen."

Now there was a round of cheers. Celia grabbed Allie's arm like a kid at a scary movie, and Allie grabbed her back. Cheerleading, thought Celia. Short full skirts and perfect matching sweaters. A gold engraved megaphone charm to wear around her neck, even when she wasn't at school. Twirling and smiling and having everyone in the school knowing that Meg and Nick weren't the only ones in this group who were important. Celia wanted it so badly she closed her eyes . . . praying that it could really, truly happen.

"Celia, are you listening?" Allie urged, her small hand still on Celia's arm.

Celia nodded.

"Girls who are interested in trying out," Mrs. Wong continued, "we'd like you to make up your own routine, since we're so rushed and still a little disorganized. Get together in groups of twos and threes for the tryouts. We'll judge you separately, but we need to see how well you can perform with a partner."

Immediately Allie's hand stretched across Celia's lap to poke Meg. "Let's try out together," Allie whispered. "The three of us." Her brown eyes were wide and excited.

"Leave me out," teased Sean from the other side. "My legs are too skinny."

Meg, meanwhile, had the flutters. Really, really bad flutters. She found it hard to sit still as Mrs. Wong backed away from the mike and Miss Meyer returned with her clipboard to give more information about honor roll, library cards, and dress code. At the same time, Allie and Celia were already writing notes to each other about cheerleading tryouts, Nick was exchanging gestures about football with a guy in the row behind him, and Sean was doodling on the cover of his math book.

Just when Meg didn't think she could take it anymore, Mr. Greer started walking up to the stage. Pink ballots were scattered on the floor in back next to Mrs. Wheeldon. Mr. Greer carried only a single piece of notebook paper.

Nick grabbed Meg's hand. Celia, Sean, and Allie leaned in. They were all breathing in the same rhythm by the time Mr. Greer marched up the wooden stairs and handed his sheet to Miss Meyer.

"We have the results of the election," Miss Meyer said as Meg doubled over so her long braid flopped down against her knees. Nick's grasp grew tighter, and Allie was whispering, "Meg McCall, Meg McCall," over and over.

"The first freshman class president at Redwood High for the Class of '88 is. . . ."

Meg bit her lip and held her breath. Time was stretching like a piece of saltwater taffy. It was taking forever for the words to come out of Miss Meyer's mouth.

Then Meg heard an "M" sound, and before she could digest that her name had actually been called, her back was being slapped and her braid tugged. Nick was pulling her to her feet, and all around her the familiar faces from Portola Middle School were applauding and waving their arms.

"YOU WON!!!"

"I knew it!"

"Oh, Meg!"

BRRIIINNNNNNNGGG. . . .

The bell rang and the five of them came together for a group hug. Then Meg grabbed her notebook and ran up to join Miss Meyer on the stage. Seats snapped up, the auditorium became a push-pull of activity, and a second later the aisles were so packed it was impossible to get through in any direction.

Celia sat back down to wait for the crowd to clear. She suddenly felt a little droopy. It was that slightly weak feeling she always got when Meg or Nick had one of their terrific successes. Already kids were crowding around the stage, trying to talk to Meg and volunteer for the fundraising committee. And somehow Meg managed to take control and yet acknowledge each and every one. It was amazing — like the way she managed to look so pretty and special in her tomboyish jeans and plain T-shirt and absolutely no makeup.

"I guess Meg won't be able to try out with us now," Allie said as she collected her books and adjusted her plastic bracelets.

Celia smiled as her best friend brought her back. "Yup. It's just you and me, but we can do it, Al."

"I know!" Allie gasped. "We can use that routine we learned when we took that dance class at Sequoia Park in seventh grade. I still remember it."

"Really?"

"Sure! See. One, two, three, four. . . ." Allie began hopping and kicking, and Celia was immediately with her. Arm over shoulder, they stepped together in time, kicking the seats in front of them and turning their heads. Celia let herself go, not caring that people were trying to get by so they could sign up for clubs and catch their buses. Some big guy bumped Allie, and she almost fell down, but she kept going until she started laughing so hard that she couldn't continue. And neither could Celia because, as usual, Allie's laugh was contagious. Celia was doubled over, too.

But Allie suddenly froze. She pointed toward

the center aisle. "Who's that?" Allie said, her laughter ceasing.

Celia looked over and her giddiness ended, too. Nick was backing toward them with a girl in a red and blue argyle sweater and knife-pleated skirt. She had a heart-shaped face, full, shoulder-length dark hair, and soft gray eyes. The girl's skin was perfect and her mouth a rosy red pout.

"Celia, Allie, this is Whitney Hain," Nick said, bringing Whitney over.

Celia wiped a smudge off her skirt. She noticed that Allie was self-consciously playing with her bracelets. Sean took one look at Whitney, stacked his books, and took off up the aisle.

"Celia's my cousin, and Allie's one of my oldest friends," Nick explained as he scooted closer. "I met Whitney this summer at one of those parties for my dad." Nick glanced back at Whitney. "My dad told me to look out for you."

There was a pause as Whitney removed a tortoise shell headband from her fluffy hair, shook her head, then reslid the band into place. When she finally extended her hand to shake, Celia saw that Whitney wore three Swatch watches, of different patterns, on the same wrist. Celia wondered if they all told the same time.

Not sure what to do, Celia shook Whitney's small hand. Allie just stood there, fiddling with her plastic charms and staring at the floor.

Nick sensed the discomfort and smiled at Whitney. "My dad said I should introduce you to Celia and my friends, since you went to Oakwood Private. I guess he figured you wouldn't know as many people as we do."

"Thank you, Nick," Whitney replied huskily.

Oakwood. Of course, thought Celia. She'd seen girls like Whitney at those parties for Nick's father, or shopping in San Francisco. It wasn't just that Whitney was beautiful — sometimes Celia suspected that she was almost as pretty as girls like that. It was something about the way this girl's eyes looked so steady and confident.

There was a long pause as Whitney smiled at Nick. Celia tried not to stare at Whitney's clothes. Finally Allie tugged on Celia's sleeve. "Let's go. I have to be out by the flagpole. My mom's picking me up."

Nick backed up, too, as if he was glad for an excuse. Boys in the back were waving him over. "I've got to talk to those guys about football tryouts."

Allie fled up one aisle and Nick the other. But Celia lingered.

Whitney took a step toward her. "I saw you dancing with your friend," she said.

Celia tensed. "So?"

"You're a good dancer, that's all," Whitney replied.

Now Celia was embarrassed. Whitney's gray eyes looked sincere. And if you thought about it, Celia reminded herself, there was no real reason why Whitney should be a snob just because she *had* money — any more than that Celia should be a lowlife because she didn't.

"You'd make a great cheerleader," Whitney added.

Celia stood a little taller. She'd always been

graceful and limber. She *would* make a good cheerleader.

"Thanks," Celia said with more warmth.

"I wanted to ask you something." Whitney's eyes clouded and her mouth fell. "No, never mind. You have all your old friends from Portola. You wouldn't want to. . . ."

"What?"

"Oh, I wanted to try out for cheerleader" — she paused — "but I don't have anyone to try out with."

Celia gulped. Could Whitney Hain be asking her to be her partner for cheerleading tryouts? Celia couldn't believe it.

"What about other girls from Oakwood?"

Whitney put her hand on Celia's wrist. Her nails were unpolished but perfectly manicured. "None of them are good enough. When I saw you dancing . . . I know you were just fooling around, but I thought we'd look so good as partners."

Celia felt as if she were being lifted off her feet. Whitney hadn't thought she was a fool, she was impressed by her! But then Celia looked to the back of the auditorium and spotted Allie, who was leaning against the double doors, waiting.

"I told my friend Allie I'd try out with her," Celia said, gesturing, "but I'm sure you could try out with us, too."

Whitney looked back at Allie, too, and wrinkled her nose. Allie was nervously chewing her nails. She was wearing those electric blue culottes, and for the first time, Celia noticed that all that plastic jewelry looked a little silly.

"No, thanks," Whitney smiled tightly. She started to leave. "I'd rather try out just the two of us. Easier to practice. You know."

Celia hesitated. "I couldn't do that. I promised Allie."

"I understand." Whitney went up the aisle, joining two other Oakwood girls. "If you change your mind, let me know," she called back. "We'd be an unbeatable combination."

Celia stared after Whitney and the other Oakwood girls until Meg trotted down from the stage and joined her.

"Who was that?" Meg asked as soon as she came over. She wasn't sure why, but something about Whitney bothered her.

"Whitney Hain. She's a friend of Nick's."

"She must be from. . . ."

"Oakwood," they both whispered at the same time, then laughed.

Meg wiped thoughts of Whitney out of her head and looked for Nick. "Where'd everybody go?" Meg asked. "I thought we were going to get together right after this and figure out where to meet tomorrow morning."

Celia didn't respond. She was still gazing after Whitney.

Meg finally spotted Nick. He was having a rowdy conversation with two Portola jocks in the back. Sean was nowhere in sight, but Allie was still waiting alone by the double doors. Meg wanted to call them all together to make plans. But before she could yell, she was interrupted by

Lisa Williams, a mousy blonde from her English class.

"Meg, I have an idea for the fundraiser. Want to hear it?"

"Sure," Meg said, trying to sound friendly.

Lisa babbled on about a bake sale and a car wash. Meg tried to act as if she were listening. It took Lisa forever to explain the most obvious suggestions, all ideas Meg had already discarded.

By the time Lisa was finished and Meg looked up again, Allie was heading out the door, and Celia was wandering up the opposite aisle. And Nick was gone, too.

CHAPTER
4

A few days later on a Friday afternoon, after the seniors' cars had squealed out of the parking lot and even most of the teachers' Volkswagens and Plymouths were gone, Allie was still at Redwood looking for Celia.

It was crazy, but then the whole week had been confusing. Allie had started out really enjoying Redwood, but on Tuesday she'd accidentally marched into the middle of a junior health class, while the teacher was holding up a clear plastic model of a woman's torso. Amid great hoots of laughter, Allie had slowly backed out the door. Wednesday had been almost as nutty. Allie had brought her clothes for PE only to find that her mother had gotten mixed up and put her little brother's shorts in the gym bag. Even though they were too small, her teacher had made her wear them anyway.

Today had been going better — the only really

weird things were some sophomores who had intentionally cut in front of her in the cafeteria line, and a senior girl who had laughed at her Gumby barrettes. But that was before school was out . . . which was a while ago. Right now she was supposed to be meeting Celia so they could work on their cheerleading routine and then go over to Meg's and make cookies. Celia had said to meet her by the fence. But which fence? There was a wire fence around the stadium, one separating the parking lot and the fields, even one between the baseball diamond and that weird old farm house on the back end of campus. Allie had seen plenty of fences, but no Celia.

Hmmmm. It was getting so late. Allie could only think that she was at the wrong fence, and that Celia had grown impatient when Allie didn't show up and had gone on to Meg's by herself. Deciding to check out the other fences one more time, Allie turned around and headed across the campus.

She wandered behind the gym and followed an unfamiliar walkway until it ended. Before her lay a square of undeveloped school land with tall field grass and that funny old Miller farm house. It looked so out of place against the new school, yet Allie found herself stepping into the high grass and over clumps of rocks and dirt to get closer. She couldn't remember if the farm house was off limits or not, and even though it made her nervous to be there, she was curious. . . . Impulse without sense, her father called it.

Allie looked around. The only people in sight were the gardeners over by the quad and the

36

football hopefuls starting laps around the baseball field. Why not at least try the door? She climbed onto the old yellow porch and pulled the squeaky screen. When it swung open easily, she pushed on the heavy wooden door behind it. That *whooshed* open, too.

Cautiously, she leaned in. Something that felt like a cobweb brushed her face — yuck! Nevertheless, she took a tiny step forward. "Hello?" she called.

"Quick, shut the door!"

The sharp male voice made Allie jump. She raised a palm to her mouth and just managed to swallow a scream.

"Close the door! Please!"

Automatically, Allie pulled the door shut behind her. As soon as it was closed, she wished she'd left it open. It was pitch black, and she was aware of someone else moving in the room. She slowly reached for the door handle, hoping to slip back out, when a bright light flicked on.

Allie blinked hard. She was standing in a wood-paneled living room that reminded her of a ski lodge or a hunting cabin. There were a few pieces of old upholstered furniture and a moose head on the wall next to a couple of white umbrellas.

But even more startling than the moose or the umbrellas was the slender boy standing at the other end of the room. He had thick, almost bristly brown hair that was cut very short so that one tuft stood up in front, almost punk. His skin was fair and his body pretty lanky, although that was a little hard to tell since he was wearing baggy clothes — old army pants with a ton of pockets and a shirt with a stenciled picture of a faded blue dinosaur.

He didn't look at her. He was totally absorbed in the camera that hung on a strap around his neck, but eventually he opened his mouth, and a voice came out.

"Sorry," he said, "I was changing film. I had it out, and I didn't want to wreck it."

He was fiddling with a lever now, turning it quickly. As he pushed on a silver button, he threw back his elbow and knocked over a light, which stood on a stand behind him.

"Oops."

When he went to pick that up, he hit his head on the handle of the white umbrella that hung from an overhead shelf.

"Ouch."

He reached up but the umbrella came tumbling down, falling over the light, which just missed smashing on an old wooden coffee table. He finally stopped trying to prevent calamity, and simply sank down into an overstuffed chair, his face in his hands.

"Darn."

Allie felt as if she were watching an old Charlie Chaplin movie. "I hope I didn't ruin your film," she said. Usually she was shy meeting new people, especially boys. But this boy seemed so laden with troubles that it took her self-consciousness away.

He finally looked at her. His face was narrow with a straight nose, and the eyes were now sweet and curious. When he smiled — a very embarrassed, but good-natured smile — Allie decided that he was cute . . . even interesting-looking. Or maybe it was just that she was so glad to meet another freshman who was even more inept than she was.

He scratched his short hair, looked around confusedly, then shot up and over to Allie. "Hope I didn't scare you." He stuck out his free hand. He had a way of moving suddenly, almost jerkily, that made Allie want to giggle. "I'm L.P. Brubaker."

"L.P.?"

"Yeah, you know, like long-playing record albums."

Allie giggled.

"Actually it stands for Leland Patterson." He made a face. "That's why I go by L.P."

"Oh. I'm Allie Simon. That's all — just Allie Simon."

"That's enough." He shook her hand with a very firm grip. "I was taking a picture of the moose. If I got the light just right I figured it would seem like the moose was looking out the window. So I set it all up, and then I realized I was out of film. And then the new roll was defective or something, so I took it apart to load it. . . I guess I shouldn't have tried to. . . ."

As quickly as he'd started this rush of conversation, he stopped, then he smiled again, only this time it was more humorous and confident. "Are you in Pittman's photography class, too?"

Allie shook her head no.

L.P.'s face grew puzzled. "Then what are you doing here?"

"Just exploring."

"Hmm." L.P. reached in his pocket and pulled

out a small slip of pink paper. "You're supposed to have a pass to come in here." He suddenly gave her a very serious look, then he grabbed his sweater from off the sofa and tossed it over the moose's snout. "He won't tell."

Allie put her fingertips to her mouth. Something about this boy made her famous giggles start to bubble. With that silly lightness brewing inside her, she took a deep breath and saluted the moose.

"Thanks."

She smiled and L.P. smiled back. They both looked away shyly. For a moment it was silent.

"This place is kind of weird," Allie finally said, eager to keep the conversation going.

"I guess they might tear it down pretty soon." L.P. shot over to a wooden staircase and gestured upstairs. "You should see the rest of it, though. There's a basement right below us, and there are all these little rooms upstairs and off that way." He pointed to his left. "One room has this painting of some old man — must be Miller, who owned this place when it was a ranch. It's creepy. He looks a lot like the moose."

Allie giggled again. "Maybe his ghost is here."

"It looks like that kind of a place, doesn't it?"

Allie closed her eyes. Immediately her imagination went wild. Goblins flying out of the fireplace, apparitions gliding down the stairs.

"I'll tell you, I've heard some weird sounds," L.P. said in a low voice. "Listen."

Allie listened, her insides all jumpy and taut — highly strung, as her mother always said. For a moment there was only a slight shuffling, her own breathing, and the buzzing of some kind of insect.

40

Then she heard it, a high-pitched beeping — halfway between an old music box and an other-worldly hum. "What's that?" Allie cried, her eyes popping back open.

L.P. took a step closer. "It's the ghost of . . . ghost of. . . ." He paused dramatically and looked around the room. His eyes wide, he finally raised his wrist — ". . . my watch!"

He pressed a button on his watch, and the electronic tune went off again.

Allie let her giggle go. She was now so wound up there was no holding back. She usually let herself get like this only in front of her little brother or her old friends, but after the nuttiness of this first week, she really needed a blow-out. Her giggles filled the low-ceilinged room until at last, panting, her laughter stopped.

"Sorry," she explained to L.P., who was staring at her and looking amazed. "I get like this some-times."

L.P. smiled and started to pack up his gear. "That's okay. It's probably a bad idea to take anything too seriously." Tugging at the bottom of his dinosaur T-shirt, he addressed the moose. "Don't you agree?"

Allie leaned against a wooden bench and watched him fold the umbrellas and collapse the aluminum light. "Definitely," she agreed. "Like this week. Starting a new school is crazy, and being a freshman isn't all it's cracked up to be." Allie found it was easy to bring the subject up; she was so sure that L.P. not only understood her feelings, but shared them himself.

"I know." Now his back was to her as he fiddled and folded.

"It's so hard to find stuff, but those upperclassmen just look at you like 'don't ask me for help.' It's like they think we're just peons. They all have short memories."

L.P. suddenly slung his camera case over his shoulder and faced her. His face was truly serious. "Wait a minute. That's not fair. I think we remember what it's like. It was only a year ago."

"What was only a year ago?"

"That I was a freshman."

Allie's giddiness went as dull as a flat Coca-Cola.

"You mean you're not a freshman?"

"You thought I was?" L.P. straightened up. He looked insulted. "I'm a sophomore."

"Sorry. I guess I made a mistake."

"Yeah, I guess you did."

L.P.'s tone was very cool. Allie folded her arms. Neither one of them said anything.

Finally, L.P. cleared his throat. "Look, I know it's hard when you're brand-new and don't know anything."

Allie felt her insides coil like a snake. She flew around and glared at him. "You're just as new to this school as I am!"

L.P. turned a shade of red. "Well, yeah, but I'm a little older."

"So what? This house is older and look what kind of shape it's in!"

L.P. just stared at her, his mouth an O of surprise, his fingers holding tightly to his camera. "Well, look, I'm sorry."

"You can be new to a place and not be a jerk," was the only thing Allie could manage to say, and somehow after she'd said that, it made her feel worse.

"Well, so much for class-to-class relations," L.P. said in a sarcastic voice.

"Yeah, so much for that," Allie echoed right back.

Both of them headed for the front door at the same time, and all they managed to do was bump into each other. It was a terrible bump — they bounced off each other as though they had been repelled by an electric current. When they finally made it to the porch, neither one of them was speaking; Allie went one way, L.P. the other. There were no good-byes and no so longs, only the muttering that came under Allie's breath as she walked back through the long grass.

"Jerky sophomore."

CHAPTER 5

"You told Allie you'd try out with her," Meg stressed. "You can't change your mind now." She was standing in the middle of her kitchen, staring at Celia and thinking how this should not be happening. It was stupid, selfish, and unfair.

"Allie's a klutz," Celia said coldly. "If I try out with her, I won't have a chance."

Meg felt like she had been punched. Celia stood across from her at the counter, staring out the window and saying impossible things as if she really believed they were true. Allie a klutz. . . ? Well, sure, she wasn't Mary Lou Retton, but then who was? If Meg remembered right, Allie had taught both girls plenty of steps. No, that wasn't the core of Celia's problem. . . . It was something else.

"I just can't do it with her," Celia finally repeated.

Meg pulled a sack of sugar down from an

overhead cabinet, shoved aside a few potted herbs, and plopped the sack on the counter. She told herself to be reasonable. She told herself that Celia wanted advice.

"Mrs. Wong said they're judging you separately" — she tried hard to smile — "so it won't matter."

"It'll still make a difference. Besides," Celia finally admitted, "I already told Whitney I'd be her partner."

Meg dropped a metal measuring cup onto the floor and turned around to face Celia. Her face now glowed as scarlet as her red track shorts and jersey. "When?"

"Today after lunch."

"Are you going to tell that to Allie?"

"I was going to tell her right after school today. We were supposed to meet by the gym, but when I saw her waiting for me . . . I didn't know what to do."

I can't believe this! Meg found herself thinking. What did Celia expect her to say? It's okay. It's great. Go ahead and try out with Whitney and just put Allie back up there on a shelf with all the rest of the things you left behind in middle school — the thrift store trinkets you used to collect, the bike you used to ride, the tree house. . . .

Meg picked up the measuring spoons and tossed them in the sink. The counter was cluttered with pottery, plants, jars of pasta, dried beans, and every possible kind of flour. Usually Meg loved the artsy clutter of her mom's kitchen, but she suddenly felt as if it were all closing in on her, making it hard for her to think. She tried again.

"You'll just have to tell Whitney that you'll only try out with her if Allie's with you, too."

"I tried that. Whitney won't do it unless it's just the two of us."

"Well, Whitney's wrong. Tell her no."

"But I already said. . . ."

"Just say you changed your mind."

"But I can't. . . ."

"You have to."

Meg froze and put a finger to her lips. Through the window she saw Allie turning the corner and coming up the sidewalk. Allie was gesturing with one hand as if she were talking to herself. In her bright pink and yellow outfit she stood out like a cartoon. Even Meg could see how Whitney was elegant and sophisticated by comparison. But so what? she found herself thinking. So stupid what!

"She's coming," Meg warned.

Celia raised herself a little to peer out the window, then flopped down in the breakfast nook and nestled her face in her arms. When Allie burst in the front door, Celia did not lift her head.

"Hi, guys," Allie said. She dropped her books in the hall, marched right over to the table, tore open the package of Ghirardelli chocolate, and popped a few chips in her mouth. She patted the top of Celia's blonde head. "I'm sorry I didn't meet you, Cici. I must have gone to the wrong fence. I waited forever and then figured you must be here."

Allie waited for a reaction from Celia. When none came, she addressed the rest of her gush to Meg. "You won't believe what happened. I went over to that farm house and met this sophomore named L.P. — like a record. He was really cute, but boy, was he a snot."

"That's nice, Al," Celia finally responded.

"Celia, I'm telling you, it was so weird. The whole place was dark when I went in, and there he was, taking pictures. I guess he has photo with Pittman. Cici, are you listening?"

Celia buried her face even more. She was already wedged between Meg's mother's homemade pottery and a stack of Xeroxed papers advertising Meg's dad's landscaping firm, and she squirmed even further into the corner, as if she were trying to disappear. "I'm listening. You met some guy. And you have a crush on him."

"I do *not* have a crush on him. He was sort of a jerk. I just talked to him in that old farm house place on campus."

Celia gave a tiny sigh. "Oh. Sorry."

Meg, who kept looking back and forth between Celia and Allie, walked over from the sink and put the bowl between them. "Why don't you two finish the cookie dough?"

Celia looked up and took a wooden spoon and stirred as Allie measured and poured the flour. Meg brought over a Pyrex bowl with the shortening and sugar, which Celia stirred and mashed. As the batter came together, Meg picked up the chocolate bag and dribbled in the chips.

"Anything exciting happen to you today, Meg?" Allie asked. She was picking the chips out of the batter and eating them almost as fast as Meg could pour them in. As she did, her plastic bracelets clattered and clicked.

Should I tell her? she wondered. Should I

bring it up right here? Unh-uh, a voice told her. This is Celia's business, and Celia is going to have to face her alone.

"Well, what do you think of the upperclass guys?" Allie chattered on, "Even though that L.P. guy was semi-jerky, I have to admit some of the sophomores are pretty cute."

"All I've been doing is trying to come up with an idea for this fundraiser," Meg answered as she grabbed the bowl of dough away from Celia and took it over to the other side of the table. She started spooning it out onto the cookie sheets in messy splats.

Celia finally lifted her head. She still wouldn't quite look at Allie, but she halfheartedly joined into the conversation. "Meg never notices guys," Celia teased. "Mark Coffield could walk by, and she wouldn't even look." Mark was a gorgeous senior who was sure to make first-string quarterback. In one week at Redwood, practically every girl in school was in love with him.

Allie giggled and put a hand over her eyes. "Go away, boys. I don't see a thing," she teased, imitating Meg. "I'm too busy planning my fundraiser."

Meg took the dough-covered spoon and gave Allie a thwack. A blob of uncooked goo landed in Allie's short, wispy hair. "I notice guys," Meg protested, trying to sound cheerful. "I just don't drool over them all the time like you two goons."

Celia and Allie laughed. That was good. Meg encouraged Allie. "So tell me more about this guy . . . LTD, or whatever his name was."

"Why do you keep asking me about him?"

Allie filled the second cookie sheet. "Actually, I did think he was cute at first. But he's a snob, and we kind of argued. But that house was so amazing. It was scary. I told L.P. it looked like it should have ghosts." Allie picked a plug of dough out of her hair. "I think L.P. thought I was a total geek."

Celia gave the slightest audible huff. "I'm sure it wasn't really scary, Al. You know, it would be better if you did try to be a little more mature sometimes."

Allie looked down, her face reflecting the hurt she felt at Celia's sudden criticism. Meg turned back from the oven and glared at Celia. But Celia just huffed again and put her head back down.

Allie sat up. "It was creepy! It's dark and old and there's this moose over the fireplace. It looks sort of like a haunted house."

"Yeah. Right."

"No, really it did. There were cobwebs and all kinds of stuff. There were. . . ." Suddenly Allie's big eyes grew even bigger, and a slight glow spread over her pale, round face. She brought her hands together, almost flapping, the way she did when she was on a laughing jag. But she wasn't laughing. She was kneeling on the kitchen chair, her mouth open as if she'd just seen a flying saucer. Even Celia had pulled herself out of her stupor to stare at her.

"What?"

"Allie, what is it?"

Allie clasped her hands together and looked at the ceiling. "That's it. That's it!!"

Meg and Celia looked at one another. "That's what?"

"The fundraiser!" Allie shrieked. "What about a haunted house? The fundraiser is right before Halloween! We could decorate that old farm house and have people play ghosts and stuff and charge admission and. . . ." Just as quickly as she'd lit up, her features went dark. "Oh, I don't know. Maybe it's a dumb idea. Too dumb."

But Meg had slid down along the kitchen cabinets until she plopped on the linoleum. "No, no, it's brilliant. It's just what we need. It's perfect!" She looked over at Celia. "Don't you think so, too? Isn't Allie brilliant?"

Celia nervously twisted a hank of hair between her fingers, nodded, and put her head back down.

An hour later the whole house smelled of cookies.

"Give these to Nick," Meg said, handing a bag of cookies to Allie. They stood in the entryway and listened to the insistent honking of Allie's father, who had just pulled up outside. Celia still sat at the kitchen table, staring grumpily in front of her. So far she hadn't said anything to Allie about cheerleading, and Meg could only hope that meant Celia had changed her mind.

"Did you save some for Sean?" Allie checked.

Meg nodded.

"So you really think my idea is good, about the haunted house?"

"Great! I'm going to present it to Miss Meyer tomorrow."

Allie gave Meg a hug, then leaned around the doorway. " 'Bye, Cici. When do you want to get together to work on cheerleading again?"

Finally Celia pulled herself out of her gloom and stood up. Meg was giving her don't-do-it looks, but Celia ignored her. She grabbed Sean's paper plate of cookies and stared out at the street. "I guess I'll take these across the street to Sean," she said in a funny voice. "Al, I'll walk you out to the car."

Meg stayed inside as the other two girls walked straight ahead. Dusk was just starting to fall, and there was a rustle of leaves and a smooth, cool breeze. Allie waved to her father, who sat waiting for her in his Volvo. As she started down the steps, Celia stopped her.

"Al, I have to tell you something."

Allie gestured for her father to wait and faced her best friend.

"Yeah, Cici, what is it?"

"Al, I guess you'll really want to be working on the fundraiser with Meg, right?"

"Sure. Especially if they use my haunted house idea." Allie stared into Celia's face. She wondered why Celia was looking so upset, and she smiled and walked her fingers up Celia's arm. It was an old joke about the itsy-bitsy spider routine that Allie's grandmother still did to her, even though she was fourteen. It was a surefire way to make Celia laugh, but this time Celia moved her arm, flicking Allie's hand away.

"Because I was thinking. . . ." Celia's voice trailed off and she looked up, biting her lip.

"What? Cici, what is it?"

"Well, I just don't see how you can help Meg and try out for cheerleader at the same time."

Allie took a step back and wrinkled her nose. Was that what Celia was so upset about . . . that Allie would get too involved in the fundraiser and not give enough time to learning a routine?

"Cici, don't worry. You know me — I'll do anything. And everything." She giggled. "I may not do it well, but I always try."

"That's just it," Celia stressed. "If you can't do something really right, then you shouldn't do it at all. Meg needs you on the fundraiser. . . ." She hesitated.

"I can do both."

"No, you can't."

"Sure, I can."

"Allie."

Something clenched inside Allie. She stared at Celia's face again and a dampness broke out over her skin. "Is it that you don't want to try out with me? Is that it?"

Finally Celia looked at her. "No, of course not. It's just that I know you'll be busy, and Whitney asked me if I'd try out with her. She doesn't know very many girls here, and she wanted to try out with just the two of us, so — "

"That girl from Oakwood Private?" Allie thought Celia might ramble on forever if she didn't stop her. "And you said you would?"

Celia shrugged.

"But what about me?"

Allie felt the tears pushing. She cried so easily — a teacher scowling at her, someone laughing behind her back, a boy she liked ignoring her hello — those prompted tears as uncontrollable as her laughter. Not wanting Celia to see how hurt she was, she backed up and headed for the car.

Celia followed her. "You understand, don't you, Al? You're still my best friend. Your haunted house idea will be a big hit, and now you'll get to make sure it's done right."

Allie swallowed back her tears, holding them down with a clench and a gulp. "Forget it, Cici."

"Al."

"It's okay."

"Are you sure?"

"Honest," Allie lied, hiding her face. "I didn't want to try out anyway." She ran down the walkway, got into her father's car, and slammed the door.

CHAPTER
6

Sean and Allie were heading over to the science labs for their last class. The two of them passed through the long grass near the old farmhouse, which they now called "the Haunted House," and trudged past two rows of newly planted rose bushes and a few heaps of what smelled like peat moss. Further off were the art bungalows and the low, square clump of science buildings, a greenhouse — still minus the windowpanes — and the gym and playing fields. It had rained the day before and the whole campus was looking soggy. Sean, who had four books under each arm and a huge wad of gum in his mouth, cut in front, twirled around, and then blew a bubble at Allie.

"Don't smile, Allie. You're as grumpy as you were the first week of school after you met that guy, what was his name? RC? R2D2?"

"L.P. Sean, leave me alone."

"Hey, Al, why did the freshman cross the road?"

"Sean!"

"Because he was stapled to a chicken."

"Sean, shut up!"

"I'm just trying to make you feel better."

"The last thing I need today is you cheering me up," she grumbled. "Wait a second, there's Meg."

Meg had just left the Haunted House and was walking down the steps and waving both her arms trying to get their attention. By the time she reached them, Meg was looking triumphant. "It's finally all settled," she told them. "Haunted House, here we go!"

"You mean they agreed?" Sean wondered.

Meg's cheeks flushed a healthy pink as she nodded and strands of shiny dark hair came loose from her French braid. "Miss Meyer got approval from the principal for almost all our ideas. There's a ton to do — I was in there last period on my study hall — but it'll work. Anyway, *we did it*!"

"That's great!" Sean shouted.

Meg looked to Allie, expecting a cheer, a hug, or at least an infectious giggle. Nothing came. "Allie, aren't you excited? Everybody's talking about what a great idea you had. I bet we raise tons of money for the stadium lights."

She waited, and at last Allie displayed the slightest smile. Considering that Allie was the one who usually jumped and screamed at the opening credits of *Family Ties*, it wasn't much of a reaction. And no sooner had her smile appeared than Allie slipped on her turquoise sunglasses and headed back in the opposite direction toward the quad.

"Where are you going?" Sean called. He hiked

up his cords, which looked at least a size too big. "Was it my breath?" Allie ignored him. "Sorry. I promise, no more jokes."

Allie waved as if to say forget it, it wasn't worth discussing. "I just forgot my science book. See you in class."

She turned around just in time to crash into a boy who was gliding to the end of the concrete path on a skateboard. Neither one of them was hurt, but Allie looked as though she wanted to punch him. Instead she stormed off in the direction of her locker.

Sean and Meg sighed. "You'd think she'd be happy now that her idea went through," Sean said. "Oh, well."

They began walking over the mucky dirt, past new beds of flowers and an area next to the greenhouse that had been roped off to make a garden.

"I think she's just upset because she liked that guy and she never saw him again — T.P., or whatever his name is. You know how Allie gets about guys."

Meg almost turned on Sean. Why did everyone think that just because a girl was upset, she was in love with some guy? Meg knew exactly what was bugging Allie, and L.P. had nothing to do with it. It was this mess with Celia and cheerleading. Just as she had expected, Allie'd been so hurt over Celia rejecting her as a cheerleading partner that last week Meg had spent two whole lunch periods feeding Allie Kleenex while she cried in the bathroom.

Luckily, it hadn't lasted. Over the weekend the five of them had gone swimming at Nick's, and

Celia had apologized — at Meg's insistence. Allie had accepted Celia's apology and cheered up. But yesterday was the day of the cheerleading tryouts and today, after school, the results were to be posted. It still bugged Meg what Celia had done to Allie — and it didn't help that the gossip going around was that Celia and Whitney were the two freshmen to watch — but it sure made it easier to understand why Allie was being grumpy.

Meg considered explaining all this to Sean, but when he blew a huge bubble of grape gum, which exploded all over his chin, she decided to skip it. Instead, they kept walking until they reached the science labs. Sean stopped and shuffled his stack of books while Meg turned toward the gym.

"Could you give this to Nick?" Sean asked, holding out a paperback copy of George Orwell's *1984*. "We get extra credit in English if we read it. There were a bunch of copies at the library, so I thought Nick might want one. I asked the librarian if next year we were going to have to read *1985*."

Meg smiled and took the book. She and Nick shared the same last-period gym, so she could certainly give it to him.

Sean started to go, then turned back. "Maybe I shouldn't have joked so much with Allie. I hope she's not mad at me." For the first time that afternoon his voice did its familiar slide. "I hate it when things get weird between any of us."

"Don't worry," Meg soothed. "It'll take a lot more than one of your terrible jokes to break up our friendship."

Sean made a goofy face and casually placed his

57

stack of books under one arm. He almost dropped them all, but just managed to juggle them until they were all clutched precariously against his chest. "See you over the weekend."

Meg tried to laugh and headed for the gym.

Fifteen minutes later "Old Miss Snyder," the running coach, was cupping her hands over her mouth and hollering, "All right, everybody! On your marks."

Meg smiled at Nick, wiped her palms against her silky gym shorts, and leaned her weight over one leg. This was her favorite time of the day. Every gym class since the beginning of school she and Nick had raced each other. Some days this was the only time she could talk to Nick, so she really looked forward to it. Just seeing him now in his Redwood gym shorts and cut-off football jersey made her feel energetic enough to run twenty miles.

"I'm going to beat you again today, McCall," he whispered. Since starting football practice, he'd been looking even broader and more muscular.

"That's what you think." Meg grinned.

"Just like I've beat you almost every time for the last two years."

"Well, what about before that? As I recall, in sixth grade I used to beat you so bad I made you cry."

Nick playfully looked around, then nudged her with his elbow. "You just cheated."

They both got into position. It was the last day of coed jogging. As of Monday the finish on the floor of the new handball courts would be dry and they would be split up — boys to team handball, girls to field hockey. So for this last run, Old Snyder had asked for volunteers to try an extralong cross-country course. It was supposed to be almost five miles, so long they probably wouldn't get back until after the final bell.

"Get set. . . ."

Meg tensed and stole one more glance at Nick. She noticed that his hair had just been cut — probably for football — and that his summer tan was fading. Nick shook out his hands and bounced to stretch his calves.

Suddenly Snyder held up her arms. "Hold it, wait a minute."

There was a collective groan. Meg turned around. What were they waiting for? A ripple went through the crowd as the answer jogged closer and closer. Suddenly the girls began to retighten ponytails, tug on gym shorts, retuck jerseys. Even the boys shook out their shoulders and stretched a little more energetically. They were all eager to impress. Quarterback Mark Coffield was going to run with them.

"Well, Mr. Coffield," Miss Snyder said with a huff in her voice. "If you want to run with us on your free period, you can at least show up on time."

"Sorry," Mark said politely, "Coach Turner caught me on my way here." Mark quickly got into the starting line, put his head down and his hands on his hips. Meg noticed that even Nick stared at him, then altered his own stance to more closely resemble Mark's.

Without any more ado, Snyder blew her whistle. "Don't bother getting set this time. Just go. GO!" She was bellowing and motioning them forward and at the same time trying to get out of the way.

Meg plunged. Thirty pairs of feet kicked up the mud until it splattered like paint and the pack was a whirlwind of legs and elbows. Right away, Mark and two girls on the cross-country team took the lead, while Meg stayed in the second pack with Nick running along right beside her. Even though Meg only came up to Nick's chin, she was leggy enough for their strides to be even. And, after so many years of running together, they paced each other naturally — the same length of step, the same rhythmic breathing.

"Did you hear about the Haunted House?" Meg asked. She was in good enough shape that chatting was easy as they jogged past the baseball diamond and the hockey field.

Nick waved to a group of boys doing calisthenics. He was huffing ever so slightly. "Is it finally all worked out?"

Meg nodded, wiping away bubbles of sweat from her upper lip.

Nick laughed, his eyes the same bright green as the new grass. "It's a great idea. I knew Meyer'd approve it."

They reached the football stadium and ran twice around the track before heading through the parking lot and away from the school grounds. Down six blocks and they left the pavement, racing instead along the side of Barricelli's vineyard, where they followed a white arrow marked in chalk along the dirt. The pack had strung out into a line, but still Meg and Nick ran double file.

"So, when is your first football game?" Meg asked as they took a turn, following the arrows across a pasture. Nick was one of the few freshmen who'd made the Varsity team, and even though he knew he'd spend most of the season on the bench, he was really excited.

"Next Friday. Man, I hope we win." They passed two bulls who stared at them from the other side of a barbed wire fence. "We'd better win."

"What if you don't?"

Nick grabbed her arm, slowing her down. "I'll take it out on you." He grinned and ran ahead, taking the lead. When they approached a huge hill, he eased up. "We're not going up Capitola Mountain Drive, are we?"

Meg picked up the pace and smiled. "Just like in sixth grade."

Nick clowned around, pretending that his legs had just turned to rubber and that he was about to give up. Meg laughed and nudged him back. Nick might avoid things he didn't like, but once he was into them he never quit. The proof of that came when they started up the steep incline of Capitola Mountain. Nick didn't slow down.

As they ran up, they passed the fancy tasting room for the Hain winery, and Meg found herself thinking about Celia and Whitney. Celia had that same never-giving-up strain. Meg had tried to talk Celia out of trying out with Whitney, but Celia wouldn't budge. Meg didn't care if Celia's chances were better with Whitney — to Meg, friendship was more important. Meg ran on, her breathing starting to get heavy, wondering if the cheerleading results would be known by the time they got back to campus.

The hill seemed to last forever, but finally they reached the crest and flew down. The wind whooshed against their bodies as gravity pulled them faster and faster until they hit the long, flat road that led back to Redwood High. Nick suddenly turned on the speed, and Meg knew he was intent on beating her.

"Here we go," Nick challenged.

As she caught Nick's playful look, Meg decided that today was the day things were going to change. No matter how it hurt, today she was going to show Nick the bottoms of her track shoes. She got up on her toes and, with a spray of mud, took off as fast as she could.

"Hey!" Nick objected, trying to keep up.

Meg gave him a catch-me-if-you-can grin and ran faster, her heart pounding and her elbows grazing against her sides while the adrenaline pumped harder and harder. She was smiling, on the verge of laughing, even though her ribs ached and her lungs burned. The finish line grew closer and closer until all she was aware of was the ground meeting her feet, her hair flying like silk, and boys yelling and yelling.

"C'mon, McCall! C'mon!"

"Rhodes, you weenie! Catch her! Catch her!"

Nick was breathing down her neck but she was almost there. Meg felt her stomach tighten, her legs scream, and then she saw it — her foot touched down a pace ahead of his. She'd won!

Meg pulled up and slowed to a trot. Nick did the same, and somehow, even though they were both out of breath, they began laughing. A deep, satisfying laugh burst out all over as other runners congratulated them and slapped them on the back.

Then Nick was congratulating her, too. His eyes sparkled in his sweat-streaked face, and when he put his arm around her shoulder, she put hers around his. "Good run!" Meg gasped.

"Yeah, good run, McCall . . . for a girl," Nick teased, and then gave her a mock slug. Meg retaliated by grabbing him around the waist and tickling him. Nick roared with delight and swung her around by one arm the way he used to do in grade school. Then both of them were on the ground and tickling harder until they were howling and laughing and gasping for breath. Nick held her arm behind her back; her leg was clamped over his, and her cheek was pressed against his bare neck. They were still laughing, but suddenly Meg was so aware of the feel of his hot, damp skin against hers that her laughter got softer, and so did his. His hand slid down her arm until he just held her wrist, and he pulled back just enough to look into her face.

Meg was dizzy. She was still light-headed from the run and the laughter, but this was something else. Everything except Nick was a blur. All she could see clearly were his green eyes looking into hers, his flushed cheeks, the golden hair flopping over his forehead. His mouth, almost smiling, no longer laughing, so close to hers and seeming to get closer. Meg's heart was pounding ten times harder than it had when she was running up the hill. She could barely breathe.

"Nick! Nick!!"

"Nick!!!"

Everything sped up again. The harsh female voices brought it all back into focus — the sky, the playing fields, the gym, the chain link fence. Nick sat up as if he'd been jolted. He seemed confused and left Meg on the grass without a word. It was a minute before Meg could sit up and figure out what was going on. First she saw Celia on the other side of the fence. Celia's hair glowed in the sunlight, and she looked radiant. Then Meg spotted Whitney, who was next to Celia, wearing a thick sweater and a swirly plaid skirt. Whitney locked her fingers in the fence and shook it joyfully.

"Nick," Whitney was calling. "We made it! Me and Celia both! We're the only two freshmen to make cheerleader! YAYYYYYYY!!!!!"

Meg tried to call back to Celia, but no sound would come out. She wanted to get up, but she couldn't move. At first she thought it was just her exhaustion from the run, then she thought it was anger over Allie. Then, as Meg stared harder, she realized that it was something about Nick and Whitney. Meg couldn't take her eyes off them. They were facing each other on either side of the metal link fence, and Whitney was leaning toward Nick. Whitney's laugh was silvery and light, and she made Nick laugh, too. Something inside Meg wanted to yell, You can't laugh with him like that! Confused, Meg stared as she felt all the happiness rush out of her as if her body had been tipped upside down.

Meanwhile, her muscles were beginning to protest in earnest. Her legs were getting shaky and tight. Looking down she saw just how muddy and hot she was, her hair in damp clumps over her face, her jersey half tucked, and her calves splattered with mud.

"Did you hear, Meg?" Celia hollered. She was so excited she was jumping up in little split leaps, her blonde hair flying. When Meg didn't join her, Celia linked arms with Nick and Whitney and trotted toward the gym.

Meg stared until she couldn't look anymore, and she brushed the blades of grass off her hands and slumped over her legs. She was feeling light-headed and a little nauseated, when she realized that someone was standing very close and peering down at her.

"You gotta watch that," he said with a wink.

Meg looked up in total shock. It was Mark Coffield. His hair was dark and cut very short, his face red from the run, and his eyes the softest brown. There was a small scar over his right eyebrow that only made him more gorgeous. He looked at her with great amusement as he stretched over to one side.

"What?" Meg gasped. She was still confused and trembly and couldn't believe Mark, a senior, was even talking to her.

Mark laughed and looked over in Nick's direction. "Beating the guy you're crazy about. He might not like it."

"Are you talking to me?" Meg swallowed.

Mark leaned forward and tapped her on the top of the head. "Don't worry. Guys'll fall in love with girls, even if they do make 'em look like wimps."

"Nick and I are just friends," Meg insisted.

Mark laughed. "And I'm Joe Montana."

The quarterback took off in a run, joining two other players who were heading toward the field. Meg fell back on the grass. She tried to laugh, too, but no laughter came. Mark had thought that she was in love with Nick? It just looked that way because they were so close and because they knew each other so well, because they were both the leaders of the group. She looked off past the fence and saw that Nick was walking back in her direction.

But as Meg stared, something started to shut down inside. Whitney was running after Nick, catching him before he reached the fence. Then Nick was holding Whitney's arm as she, giggling, twisted it away. Whitney threw her head back and said something that made Nick laugh, and a sharp pain cut from Meg's stomach up to her chest.

Meg curled up, bringing her knees to her forehead, making herself small and hidden. Her head was throbbing, and she didn't want anyone to see her. Pressure was building in the back of her throat, and she felt as if she might start crying. She saw Nick climbing the fence again and heard Snyder yelling at him to walk around like a normal person, and then felt his warm palm on her back.

"Isn't it great," Nick was saying, "that Celia

and Whitney made it? The only freshmen." There was something about his voice that sounded a little funny, strained.

Meg was suddenly so aware of his hand against her back that she was afraid to meet his eyes. Nick had touched her a thousand times, but now his hand was too warm, his whole body much too close. When she finally did look up, he took his hand away. He seemed embarrassed.

"Meg, are you okay?" Nick nudged her. "See what happens when you have to prove how macho you are? Now you're going to throw up or something." He laughed.

Meg held herself even more tightly. A tear had just slid down her cheek.

"Hey. Meg? Honestly, are you feeling okay?"

"I'm fine," Meg said, standing as quickly as she could. She saw a few of the slowest runners just straggling in. She looked beyond at the unfinished tennis courts and fog and the green hills. She was amazed that it all looked the same when everything inside her had taken a nosedive. She put her hands to her face and brushed off the tear as if she were hot.

"You just don't want to admit that it was so hard for you to beat me." Nick laughed. His laughter sounded funny, unnatural. He started to go, then hesitated. For a moment they stared at one another until Nick got that embarrassed look again and turned away. "Meg, I have practice now. Are you sure you're okay?"

Using every ounce of will, Meg made herself look as if nothing were wrong.

"Don't get cocky," he teased, running off toward the stadium. "Next time, I win."

Meg watched him go. As she did, she knew that everything Mark Coffield had said was true. Maybe that was why the tree house had been so important to her. She was in love with Nick. In love with him. And now that she knew that, nothing in her life would be the same.

CHAPTER 7

Five.
Four.
Three!
Two!
One!

There was a huge cheer. Students and cheerleaders rushed onto the field. Backs were slapped.
Players were lifted up onto students' shoulders.
The band broke out into the school fight song, and
even the Petaluma mascot — a scrungy-looking
billy goat — was bleating for victory.

But on the other side of the field — the Redwood Grizzly side — there was almost total
silence.

"We got creamed. First game of the season
and we got creamed." Nick pulled his helmet off
and shook his head in disbelief. There were dirt
and grass stains all up and down his brand-new

uniform and what felt like bruises from his ankles to his chin. Slowly, dejectedly, he followed the other guys and headed off the field.

"Nick, Nick . . . wait up!"

It was Whitney and Celia in their blue and red cheerleading outfits, standing just inside the fence. They each held a pair of pom-poms under one arm, and Whitney was still shaking hers half-heartedly. Before the game, the sight of them in their new twirling skirts and lettered sweaters had made him feel as if the team would tear down the goal post, but now that they were bruised and crushed and beaten . . . well, it made him feel slightly sick.

But he had to do something, so he waved and put his head down, intending to hurry into the locker room. Too late. They rushed up beside him, Whitney reaching him first.

"You were wonderful," Whitney clamored.

Nick was amazed that she was looking at him as though she actually meant it. "Right," he scoffed. "They killed us."

"Fourteen to nothing isn't so bad."

"The nothing is what hurts."

"It's okay, Nick," Celia offered. She knew better than to try and cheer him up. "You did your best."

Do your best . . . do your best . . . that's what Nick's dad always pushed for. For once Nick was glad that his dad spent so much time out of town. At least he hadn't witnessed his youngest son finally getting in the game the last quarter and then twice being thrown for a loss.

Celia seemed to read his thoughts and gave him

a sympathetic look, but Whitney was still smiling at him as if he'd just won the Super Bowl. Patting his back, Celia said in a businesslike voice, "Nick, I'm supposed to eat dinner at your house tonight. Remember? If you want, I'll wait for you and we can walk together."

Nick shrugged. He wasn't sure what he wanted to do — go in and mope with the other guys, get yelled at by the coach, or walk home silently with Celia. None of it appealed to him. He kicked the grass and headed for the gate.

But before he could go through, Whitney whipped in front of him, put her hands on her hips, and gazed into his eyes.

"Nick, I don't care what you say. You really were terrific. I loved watching you."

Nick stared off at the brand-new bleachers. Paper cups and crumpled papers dotted the perfect wood and concrete.

Whitney took another step in. Her fluffy hair was being tossed by the breeze, and she pushed it away from her face with both hands. "When you got the ball from that huge Petaluma guy and ran with it — that was the most exciting moment of the game."

Nick shrugged. Maybe, he thought. That was the one time in the game when he'd at least done something right. Even if he had only gained two yards.

"The other guys just weren't backing you up."

Whitney's voice was soothing and sweet, and for just a moment it felt good to believe her. Since the beginning of school, she'd been coming up to him at lunch, before practice, between classes.

She would look at him with those gray kitten eyes and stand so close that Nick was beginning to miss his shadow. Her curves were nice, though, and she did have those pretty eyes. . . .

"Who cares? We just lost, that's all." Nick jerked himself back to reality and then turned to go. But before he knew it was happening, Whitney stopped him, got up on her tiptoes, laced her arms around his neck, and pressed her cheek to his. Nick was very aware of his sweat and the dirt, but heck . . . if she didn't mind. . . . She clutched behind his neck and buried her face against his shoulder. Boy, did she smell good, and her hair was so soft. When Whitney finally let him go, he stepped back on one cleat, tottered, and grabbed the fence for balance.

"Thanks." He had no idea what else to say.

Now Whitney's rosebud mouth was in a great big smile. Her cheeks were even more flushed than before. "Nick, I've been wanting to ask you — did you hear about the first dance? It's in two weeks. Are you going?"

Nick was now even more confused. Here he was, still coated with dirt, his head still light from her little tackle, and now she was bringing up the dance. Did she mean that she wanted him to ask her to be his date? He didn't want to disappoint her — he never liked to disappoint anyone. Still. . . .

But before the words could come out, he saw Coach Turner on the other side of the fence, his thick face bunched up like a bulldog. "C'mon, Rhodes. Quit flirting with the cheerleaders. Hit the showers. Move it!"

Whitney's slender shoulders slumped forward, but Nick reacted as though he'd just hit a hot wire. Ramrod straight, he backed up and eased sideways through the gate. As he did, he caught Celia's eye and noticed that his cousin looked a little embarrassed for him.

Nick started to run. "Celia, don't bother waiting for me. I'll see you at the house tonight," he yelled back. When he passed the coach, Turner gave him a stinging whack on the behind. Nick had the feeling that this was going to be one long afternoon.

But Turner wasn't as tough on them as Nick thought he would be. Maybe they all looked so pathetic and depressed that the coach couldn't bear to punish them further.

"Shake it off, guys. We'll come back," the coach bellowed later in the locker room. He patted each of them on the shoulder and then told them to be ready for a good practice tomorrow. Most of the guys headed instantly for the door, but a few lingered, snapping towels and combing their hair.

"Let's go scarf some pizza," demanded Jay Creary, a junior lineman. Jay had bragged about eating three pizzas by himself after a game.

The other guys hollered and joked, but Nick just sat there slumped on the locker room bench.

"Hey, Rhodes, forget it," stressed Mark Coffield. "It's just a game."

Nick tried to smile, but he didn't feel any better. In fact, since the girls had left he'd felt empty and alone. Suddenly he wanted to be with the people who would think the same of him whether he'd been the hero or dropped the ball. Not Whitney — she was too weird — but as he picked up his gear he wondered if Meg, Sean, and Allie were still on campus working on the Haunted House.

They'd been there after school almost every day — as often as he'd been at practice. He'd spotted Allie and Sean during halftime, and they'd warned him that because of the house they wouldn't be able to stay for the whole game. The way things had turned out it was just as well anyway, but Meg . . . well, Nick had just wanted to see her.

He'd barely talked to Meg since that last day of coed jogging. For a few days afterward he'd avoided her. Something had happened that day after the run that he didn't quite understand and wasn't ready to deal with. But he'd put it out of his mind, and they'd both been so preoccupied that he didn't have to think much about it. Now he missed her like crazy. He'd called her twice that week, but she hadn't called him back. She spent almost every lunch in the Haunted House. And just yesterday he'd yelled hello to her from across the quad, and she'd pretended she hadn't heard him.

"So, Rhodes," yelled Jay impatiently, "are we going for pizza or what? If so, let's go!"

Nick grabbed his notebook and stood up. "I'm going over to check on that Haunted House thing, see how it's coming." Jay rolled his eyes, but Terry Warner, a sophomore, let him know where to get off.

"Don't make faces, Creary. It's to raise money for the stadium lights. You want to keep playing in the afternoon forever?" He punched Jay's round belly. "Besides, you need another pizza like you need another Petaluma guy ramming your brains."

Jay laughed, a big round laugh. Terry laughed, too, and with Nick leading the way, they headed over to the Haunted House.

"Sean Pendleton, would you quit horsing around!"

Allie pushed at the rag mop that Sean was twirling in front of her face and stamped her foot. Sean could either be the smartest, most fun person in the world, or the most juvenile. Today he was at his worst. Meg had made him put on a shower cap to keep the paint out of his red hair, and an apron to protect his clothes. For some weird reason he'd gotten into the whole idea, and now he was talking about being Eddie Van Halen and was using the mop both to play guitar and poke at Allie. With all the work there was to do, she wanted to kill him.

"You are such a nerd!" she yelled again when he came forward swirling the mop.

"Nerd?" Sean said. "That's absurd," and then he poked at her again with the mop.

"Meggggggg! Would you come in here and handle this harebrain?"

Meg appeared from around the corner. She was wearing overalls and an apron identical to Sean's, but she was holding a big dripping paintbrush in one hand. She stepped over a piece of newspaper when her brush started to drip. "Sean," she smiled, "don't be a bozo. There's a ton to do."

"I know, I know," he said seriously, "and I've been doing it. I've knocked down all the cobwebs you told me about, but I don't see why. When we make this place scary we're just going to want to put them up again."

Meg sighed and wiped her forehead with her clean hand. "Okay, look," she said, "if you're done with the cobwebs you can start stirring those cans of paint." She pointed to six or seven paint cans that sat near the front door on a plastic tarp. "I think Penny and Doug are ready for a few of those upstairs."

Sean frowned and looked down sadly at his mop. He stuck it forward and pretended to play another guitar riff for the girls, but neither one of them was impressed. "Okay, okay," he said, "I was just trying to inject a little humor. You guys are so serious."

"You are so ridiculous," Allie complained. "You think you're still in Mrs. Sheffield's class in middle school."

Sean turned a little red on that one. Back in seventh grade he'd gotten a reputation as a real clown, the kid who could always be counted on to disrupt just about anything. One day he'd almost destroyed the school laboratory with a huge baking soda and vinegar volcano, and another time he'd let a lizard go in the cafeteria line — a move that made one of the cooks grab him by his ear and haul him all the way down to the principal's office. His parents had been called in; Sean still remembered with a smile how his father had listed the productive activities that he and his son had shared. They'd built a bicycle frame from scratch, survived three-week backpacking trips, even created a Dungeons and Dragons game on the store computer. If Sean could do those things so well, his father demanded, why was he having trouble with the seventh grade? Then his mother, who was perhaps the best bicycle repairperson in all Northern California, stood up and suggested in strong language that Sean was simply bored and it was the school's fault. As a result, Sean was put in an accelerated program so that he didn't have time to horse around.

Today he felt the kind of grating frustration that he used to feel in middle school. Maybe it was getting used to high school, maybe it was sitting through that football game. Sean held the mop more tightly and found his mind swimming around in a dozen different fantasies — rock star, pole vaulter, spear carrier, Olympic equestrian — there were all kinds of things that he could do with a mop. But as he clutched the wooden stick even more tightly, he thought about the one thing he couldn't be — no matter who came into the principal's office and stood up for him — and that was on the football team with Nick. No. He was about thirty pounds too light and about a hundred percent too uncoordinated.

But he didn't tell that to the girls. Instead, when Allie and Meg went back to their painting, Sean did exactly what he was supposed to do. He sat down on one of the buckets of paint and picked up two wooden stirrers. . . . Just then

77

another fantasy came into his head. If the mop had been an electric guitar. . . .

Sean carefully balanced the paint stirrers in the crook of each hand and then began tapping out rhythms. The tops of the buckets produced satisfying tings. Pretty soon he was wailing. He was in an MTV video playing behind Sting, thrashing at his bass drum and tom-toms, crashing the cymbals, hammering the cowbell. His thrashing at his bass drum and tom-toms, crashstop. With the apron and the dustcap on he decided that he was WHAM!'s new drummer and in the middle of his number had actually stood up and moved around the paint cans while he played. One step, two step, cymbals, snare, crash. . . .

THUNK!

Sean heard the front door fly open and in his dust cap and apron slowly turned around. Jay Creary and Terry Warner were both standing there like two stocky trees in their jeans and nylon warm-up jackets.

"Look at this, Rhodes," howled Jay, "it's the singing fairy." Sean backed up, trying to get away, then tripped over a partly opened can. There was a crash and black paint was suddenly oozing over his tennis shoe. Jay and Terry were laughing, but then Nick walked past them. Sean stood up straight, ignoring the paint that was dripping onto the bare floor. He was sure that Nick would shut these jerks up.

"Takes one to know one," Sean boasted, looking at Nick. "Right, Nick?"

But Nick didn't respond. Not only did Nick not defend Sean, he stood as if he were trying to look right through Sean . . . as if Sean did not exist. Sean wrapped his arms around his narrow chest, as if to make sure he was still there. Nick's coolness made him feel invisible.

"Where is everybody?" Nick asked flatly.

Sean looked around. The other students were scattered throughout the other rooms. Still, *he* was there. Nick had asked the question as if the living room were empty.

"Upstairs. In the basement."

Nick didn't say anything else and Sean looked down. Maybe it was the dumb clothes Allie and Meg had made him put on. He whipped the shower cap off his head and took off the apron. Why had he ever put on this stupid get-up? Meanwhile Terry and Jay plopped down in the two old armchairs and were staring up at the moosehead over the fireplace. Their large bodies took over the whole room.

"Do you want to see the house?" Sean asked.

Nick still didn't answer, but when he nodded, Sean headed for the staircase. He felt better that Nick was following. Good. The guys would see that he and Nick were two of a kind, inseparable.

But as Sean started up the first stair, he noticed that Nick had turned off in another direction. Sean called out to him, but his friend was gone.

Meg heard Sean's voice from the kitchen, where she was washing out brushes in the sink. There was paint in her hair and dirt on her face, and she doubted her hands would ever come clean. When she heard someone in the doorway, she turned, expecting to see Sean, but when she looked up and saw that it was Nick, her skin went hot and she felt breathless.

"Hi."

"Hi."

Nick came closer, and she realized that she was staring at him, so she looked back down at the sink and turned the water on even harder. Without a word, she concentrated on rinsing the paint from the bristles. Every tiny streak, every drop.

"Are things going okay?" Nick asked slowly.

Meg gave the slightest nod. She lifted her shoulder to clear away a smudge from her cheek, then realized that she was so coated with muck that she would probably only make herself look worse. She wanted to say something, but her heart was pounding so fiercely that it was impossible to think.

"You think you'll get everything done on time?"

"Sure." Meg washed her brushes — kneaded, rinsed, and scrubbed.

A sigh came from Nick that was so loud Meg could hear it above the running water. "Don't you even want to know how my game went?"

Finally Meg looked at him again. His hair was still wet and a little water had dripped down on his collar. She noticed that his eyes, usually bright as candles, looked tired and disappointed. His sadness flowed into her like smoke. She knew the team had lost. "How'd it go?"

"They killed us."

Meg tried to smile. In a way she really wanted to run over and throw her arms around him. She wanted to say, It's not that important! It's only a game. Let's you and I hike in the hills until the sun goes down and talk about things that really matter, then you won't even think about something as dumb as football. But of course she didn't say a word. Instead, she turned off the water and laid the brushes at the side of the sink. Tearing off sheets of paper toweling, she pressed them dry.

Nick shifted awkwardly. "Anyway, I just thought I'd stop by and see how things were going. It looks like the place is really getting cleaned up."

"It is."

Nick started to go, then reconsidered and took a step in. "Meg, are you mad at me about something?"

Meg's throat clenched up and she felt slightly dizzy. She continued to pat and dry the same brushes until the bristles started coming out in her hand. What was she supposed to say? I love you, Nick! I've probably loved you for a long time. But ever since I've figured it out I can't look you in the face without everything inside me going crazy.

"Meg! Are you mad at me?" Nick came closer. "Did I do something?"

Meg felt like she was going to sink into the floor. "No."

"Oh. That's good."

The kitchen went silent. When Meg couldn't stand it anymore, she turned the water on again and started rewashing the already clean brushes. She expected Nick to leave, but he didn't.

"The dance is coming up soon." Nick gave a funny laugh. "You gonna go?"

Meg stopped her furious scrubbing. Open-mouthed, she looked up at Nick. Her mind was going a million miles an hour, and her heart was going even faster. Was it possible that he had come to the Haunted House to find her and ask her to the dance? She felt like the room was shaking. "I guess."

"Yeah." Nick looked back toward the living room. "I guess everybody will."

The room stopped shaking, and Meg felt like she'd been thrown against the wall. He wasn't asking her. Of course he wasn't asking her. She was just his friend. Practically his sister. She was the one who held everything together, who did everything right. Compared to a girl like Whitney she was as alluring as dirt. "Listen, Nick, we have a lot of work to do, so if you're not going to help, you shouldn't hang out here."

For a second Nick's eyes narrowed, and then he thrust out his chin and held up his hands. "Sorry." He turned to go. "See you sometime."

Meg stared down into the sink and waited for him to leave. She listened to every footstep, every grunt and guffaw, as Nick and the other players trampled through the living room and out the front door. As soon as she was sure that Nick was gone, she picked up her entire tray of perfectly clean brushes and threw it down on the dirty floor.

CHAPTER 8

While Nick and Meg talked, Allie sneaked away from the Haunted House, past the greenhouse and the new plants, across the quad, through the parking lot, and away from Redwood High.

"I hate high school," she said glumly to herself.

She kicked at some stray leaves that had fallen down from a big eucalyptus and did a zigzag as she crossed the street. She just couldn't take it anymore! Sean was driving her crazy. Meg was suddenly moody and curt. Nick was acting like he'd lost his only friend, and Celia hadn't even bothered to come over after the game — she'd gone off with Whitney Hain.

"Whitney Pain is more like it," Allie mumbled as she headed in the opposite direction from the vineyards and the meadows.

Obviously Whitney thought that Allie was a creep, an immature zero. Allie had seen the way Whitney had looked up at her during halftime, as though Whitney owned the planet and Allie were just renting a room. Maybe Whitney was right. Maybe Allie was childish and dorky. After all, Whitney wouldn't use a seventh-grade dance class routine to try out for cheerleader. Whitney never laughed too loudly, or bit her nails, or put together outfits only to get to school and realize that the colors didn't really go.

Allie crossed one more street, left the residential area, and headed downtown. She could hear her father screaming at her for leaving campus, but right now, if she had the opportunity, she'd take a long voyage on a tramp steamer. Allie wished that Emily, her baby sister, would hurry and grow up so that her mother had a little more energy to see just how ridiculous her father was being. Her mom had been strict enough in the past, but her father . . . he acted like Allie was the heir to the throne or something. On the one hand there were big shots like Whitney making her feel dumb and insignificant, and on the other was her father making her feel like a very important two-year-old. Didn't anybody realize that she was a normal human being? Maybe downtown there would be people like that. She could hope.

Allie walked faster, wrapping her arms around her chest and trying not to dislodge the buttons and badges that she had pinned to her jeans jacket. Fall was in the air — a nip of cold was mixed with exhaust from the five o'clock traffic. Dodging a Coors Beer truck, Allie passed the fire station and the Albertson's supermarket until the entrance to the downtown outdoor mall came into view. It was rustic and old-fashioned with the big department stores and fast-food chains kept far away. In their place were chic clothing boutiques, specialty shops like Sean's parents' bicycle store, and cozy restaurants.

Allie knew exactly where she was headed.

At the top of the mall was a big bookstore called Bruno's. Behind Bruno's was an outdoor café where they sold pastries and Italian coffee, called cappuccino, that came in heavy white cups. The umbrellaed tables were always filled with university students and older high schoolers. Allie had been there once with Meg and Celia, but this was the first time she'd had the guts to go alone. When she got to the outside of Bruno's, she almost turned back, but she wouldn't let herself. Instead, she walked past the tall shelves of books and out onto the brick patio.

Breathing in the smell of coffee and cinnamon, Allie marched up to the order counter. She wasn't sure where to stand, or what to say, and she shriveled like an old grape when two college girls took cuts and pushed her back in the line. Still, she was going to do it — she honestly was. Everything was very cool until she felt whatever it was that was stuck under her foot and was twisting around and — *"Oh, my gosh, I'm sorry I'm stepping on your foot!"*

"That's okay. I have another one," came the reply.

Allie turned very fast because the voice sounded familiar, and she couldn't think of very many people who would say something as corny as that. Sure enough, it was him all right. Brubaker. Sophomore L.P. Allie wanted to die.

She jerked away as though she had stepped on a cat. In fact she almost lost her balance, and one of the girls who had taken cuts grabbed her arm so she wouldn't fall.

Allie nodded a voiceless thank you — even though she knew the girl didn't deserve it — and brushed her bangs out of her eyes. She turned around and L.P. was staring at her.

"Hello, again," he said.

"Hi," she managed back.

"You okay? I didn't trip you, did I?"

"No."

"I think you stepped on me first. I hope it wasn't on purpose."

"Of course not," Allie murmured. "I'm sorry." She avoided his eyes but noticed he wore those same kind of pants with tons of pockets, a baggy print shirt, and carried a canvas photographer's bag and a brown paper sack from Bruno's. His hair still stuck up in that little tuft, which Allie now found extremely irritating.

"What are you doing here?" he asked.

I have just as much right to be here as you do, she felt like saying. Just because you're a sophomore, and I'm merely an insignificant. . . . But she didn't. Instead, Allie pulled the collar of her denim jacket up around her neck and looked straight ahead. "I'm getting something to drink. What does it look like?"

"I guess it looks like you're getting something to drink. So am I."

They both faced the counter in silence. L.P. folded his arms. Allie cleared her throat and rocked back a little on her heels. She tried to look like coming down here for coffee was an everyday thing. The two girls who'd gone ahead of Allie were gone, and she was next. The counterboy was looking at her, waiting for an order, but Allie felt so self-conscious she couldn't think clearly. L.P. moved up alongside her.

"The cappuccino is great here," L.P. said.

Allie squinted at the blackboard menu. All she needed was for L.P. to know she'd never ordered by herself before. "I know."

"What would you like?" the guy behind the counter said impatiently.

L.P. looked at her, but now Allie was off balance, and the few times she'd drunk coffee it'd made her feel like she was going to jump out of her skin. Actually, she didn't really even like coffee unless she put about five spoonfuls of sugar in. But most of the other drinks had Italian names and she didn't know what they were.

"If you don't drink coffee they have these special sodas that are. . . ."

Allie propped her elbows on the metal counter and said very clearly, "Cappuccino, please."

The counterboy nodded. But before making her order he looked at L.P., as if she and L.P. were together.

"Make that two," L.P. told the counter guy, who just nodded. "And an order of biscotti."

L.P. said that with a hint of an Italian accent, which Allie thought was just another way of showing that he was really sophisticated. Still, she couldn't help being curious about what "biscotti" were. When the counterman handed L.P. a plate, she saw that they were big, hard cookies, like the ones Emily chewed on to help her teething.

The big brass machine spat out the cappuccinos, and she was reaching for her money when she heard L.P. again. He already held four dollars in his hand.

"I'll treat," he said, and then he laughed a little awkwardly when she looked at him. He gestured to his paper sack. "My book was on sale, so I'm rich. Anyway, at least I have a few dollars left over."

Allie hesitated just long enough for the counter guy to take L.P.'s money. She was shocked that L.P. wanted to pay for her, but when she thought about asking him why, he scooped his cup off the counter — the frothy milk splashing over into the saucer — and started looking for a table.

Now Allie was even more confused. She wanted a small, secluded table where she could sit alone, but nothing was available. L.P. had managed to spot a table for three in the opposite corner.

"We'd better hurry." He rushed over, plopping down just ahead of some college students. He gestured for Allie to sit across from him.

Allie slid into the chair, thinking now that it was dumb even to have come down here. She felt so uncomfortable that the idea of eating or drinking anything now was totally unappealing.

"Thanks," she mumbled.

"Well, I kind of owe you one."

"What?" Allie looked at him, puzzled, but

before L.P. could explain he took a big gulp of cappuccino. Too big. He brought a hand to his mouth, then choked and started to cough.

"Are you all right?" Allie rose and tried to pat him on the back. "Are you okay?"

L.P. coughed a couple of times, sputtered, and then nodded. Allie sat back down thinking he had recovered, but when he started turning red she became alarmed.

"Do you want some water?" Allie asked, standing up again.

He waved a hand and nodded.

Allie quickly skirted over to a nearby cart and brought him back a full glass. He took it greedily, drinking it down to the bottom before looking at her. Suddenly Allie felt herself soften. L.P.'s face had the same sweet, goofy quality that it did when she'd first seen him juggling his photography equipment. She felt herself blush and sat back down. She took a sip of coffee. A small, tentative sip.

"Are you okay?"

There were some more quiet coughs and he cleared his throat. For a second his eyes flickered up to meet hers. His face was still very red. "Thanks," he croaked in a super-low voice, and then added, "Whew."

Allie nodded and wiped away the foam that had settled on her upper lip. The steamed milk that floated on top of her coffee was thick and tasted of cinnamon. "Why did you say you owe me one?" she asked softly.

L.P. shrugged. "I heard about the Haunted House thing that your class is doing."

Allie looked up. L.P. was referring to the freshmen but this time there was no derision in his voice, no snobbery. Still, she was on her guard.

"What about it?"

"Well, a friend of mine is on the senior fund-raising committee, so he knows about all the classes' projects. Anyway, he mentioned your name, and that you had come up with an idea." He glanced at her as if waiting for her to confirm his information. "I was just glad because now the house won't be torn down, and I like that old house. Maybe I'll get to take more pictures in there after you guys are done, so" — he cocked his head and smiled — "that's why I owe you one."

Allie took another sip. Everything inside her was shifting, changing from anger and nerves to something as highly charged, but much more pleasant and warm.

"Gee, thanks."

"Sure."

"The house is starting to get cleaned up," she admitted. "You might not recognize it. You should come by some afternoon and see."

"I have come by." L.P. gave a funny laugh. "I thought maybe you'd be there so I could say I was sorry for being such a jerk that first time we met."

"You came by looking for me . . . to say you were sorry?"

L.P. shrugged.

"But I was the one who was a jerk. I was up-tight because it was my first week."

L.P. smiled and she smiled, too. This time when it went silent it didn't feel quite so awkward. Now Allie didn't want the conversation to end. She pointed to L.P.'s paper sack. "What book did you buy?"

L.P. pulled out a large slim volume, like the ones Allie's parents stacked on their coffee table. "It's about modern painters." He held it up for her to look at the cover. "Isn't that amazing?"

It was a painting of a cattle skull, in pale desert colors, eerie but very beautiful. Looking at it made her feel sad, lonely.

"It's by Georgia O'Keeffe," L.P. told her.

"It's so beautiful." Suddenly, she was embarrassed again. Her mother was always teasing her about being so emotional — impressionable, she called it — and here she was practically crying over some painting on the cover of a book. But when she met L.P.'s eye, he seemed to be appreciating her reaction.

"I know. It does that to me when I look at it, too."

Allie went back to her coffee. "Kind of reminds me of the moose in the Haunted House."

L.P. laughed and turned the book around. "It kind of does, doesn't it?" He looked up. "Hey, you're not taking the moose down, are you?"

"Unh-uh. In fact people are talking about making it our class mascot."

"Yeah. Bullwinkle, Class of eighty-eight."

They looked at each other, and Allie felt her insides start to go wacky. It was that old giggly sensation bubbling up inside. Before she knew it she heard high-pitched chuckling, and she knew it was coming from her.

"You could all wear moose horns instead of caps on graduation," said L.P. Now they were both laughing, and Allie could tell that people were staring. L.P. didn't seem to mind. He was looking at her with the happiest, most delighted eyes.

Finally Allie regained control. Her eyes were teary and she wiped them with her napkin. "Sorry," she said, looking around. The people at the table next to them had gone back to their cappuccinos.

L.P. was shaking his head. "You have a great laugh."

"No, it's awful."

"It makes me laugh just to hear it."

"It's horrible. It's so loud."

"So's Bullwinkle."

Allie felt like she might go off again. They both leaned forward over the table and the cups rattled and both pairs of their hands were stretched over L.P.'s book, but suddenly Allie's spirits tumbled. She gasped.

"What's the matter?" L.P. asked, instantly picking up her panic.

Allie was already standing. "Is your watch right?" She had just seen that it was a quarter to six. Her father was picking her up. Allie had fifteen minutes to get back to school or her father would know she'd left the campus.

L.P. checked his wrist. "I think so."

Allie quickly buttoned up her jacket. "Thanks for the coffee. I have to go."

"Listen, Allie."

"Yes."

"Did you hear about the dance? The first one. It's in a couple weeks."

Allie's heart stopped.

"I figure I'd better ask now because the way things have been going, I might not see you at school and. . . ."

"Yes!!?"

"I wondered if maybe you wanted to go . . . with me, I mean."

Allie was too shocked to answer.

L.P. tried to fill the space. "If you don't like dances, we don't have to stay long. I can drive, you know. I can get my dad's car. . . ."

"The dance?"

He nodded.

Allie had a fleeting thought that it might be a joke, but she managed to look back up at L.P., and his hopeful eyes were fixed on hers, and she knew it wasn't a joke. Allie's heart jumped and her hands trembled. She steadied them by grabbing the back of the chair.

"Yeah, I guess. I mean, sure."

"Great."

L.P. slipped the Bruno's bag toward her and held out a felt-tipped pen. "You'd better give me your phone number so I can call you and figure when to pick you up and all that."

"Okay." Allie scribbled and started to back up, almost tripping over a baby stroller and a potted palm. "Thanks."

"I'll call you. 'Bye."

" 'Bye."

She turned and took off. Racing, she left the mall, and tore back along the sidewalks until Redwood was in view. Then it hit her — the dance and L.P. coming to pick her up and what she would wear and how she would ever survive until then. She moved even faster, worrying about what time it was and if she was late and what kind of fit her father would have if she wasn't there when he arrived. But even as she ran — and worried — there was also something else. Something great and grand and terrific and wonderful. Something so big in her heart that Allie found herself thinking that high school — just maybe — wasn't so bad after all.

CHAPTER
9

Back at the farmhouse, Meg slowly shut the door and searched in her pocket for the key. The wind was beginning to blow and she could hear it running through the grass. Sean was waiting patiently — the only one left. He was holding on to three buckets of paint, and there was a smudge on his forehead.

"Can you find it?" he asked.

"I can find it," Meg said above the wind. She never lost anything. Still, she dug deeper in her pockets and all she could come up with was a quarter and a paint-spotted Band-Aid. Why that was there she couldn't guess, but after seeing Nick she was feeling so disoriented she might as well have been one of the fall leaves that were beginning to swirl around the school.

She reached deeper, standing on one tiptoe and pushing her fingers down. There it was, the key that Miss Meyer would entrust only to Meg. The adviser had made a big point of Meg's being the only freshman dependable enough to lock up. Meg pulled the key out, put it in the brass lock, and turned. The bolt clunked in.

"Let's go," Meg tried to say cheerily.

Sean squinted and attempted to wipe some paint off the back of his arm, but his hands were too full. Meg jumped off the porch and took one of the buckets from him. They stood there for a moment in the tall grass, and Meg thought of being in Africa on safari — she and Sean, big game painters.

"Thanks for waiting for me," Meg said.

"That's okay."

She patted Sean's slim shoulder. There were times when Sean's manic smarts and craziness were hard to take. But looking at him now in his green T-shirt with one pocket and the baggy blue jeans cinched tight with the beaded cowboy belt, Meg was flooded with affection for him. At times they were as close as brother and sister. When one of them was feeling really down — like Meg was now — it was almost as if the other had a special antenna. Sean was too smart and sensitive to act artificially cheerful.

They walked out of the tall grass and toward the athletic fields. The school spread out beside them like a jumble of geometric shapes with the early evening sun spiking rays between the buildings. The sunset had painted the sky red and orange and deep purple, and Meg decided Redwood Hills had to be one of the loveliest places on earth. Maybe it was the sound of the wind, or the pink clouds that rolled gently up from the ocean. Whatever it was, Meg felt such an intensity of beauty and sadness that it made her almost slow down and stop. But Sean wouldn't let her. "Let's go, Meg," he called.

They got up to the building that housed the main power generator. "This is where the janitor wanted us to leave the leftover stuff," Meg explained. She slowly lowered the heavy paint can.

Sean gave a tired shrug. "I thought maybe we'd do some graffiti."

Meg didn't respond to his joke, but the thought of MEG MCCALL WILL SURPRISE YOU ALL in big, bold letters across the parking lot at least brought a smile to her face.

Sean noticed her smile. "Nah, you'd never do anything like that, would you?" He checked the lids of the paint cans, not waiting for an answer.

He didn't have to, Meg thought. Of course she would never paint graffiti, or cut class, or dye fuchsia streaks in her hair. She was the one who took care of everybody else, who could be trusted and depended on. She was as reliable as the tardy bell and about as exciting. No wonder Nick thought of her only as a friend.

They neatly lined the cans against the door, while Meg wondered if she could explain what she was feeling to Sean. The fact that she was in love with Nick was bad enough — and since she'd figured it out, she'd been keeping it so far back in her heart that it was like the way her mother sometimes forgot food in the icebox. But there was something else that bothered her, something else that made her feel chilled and left out. Meg was tired of being the one who held things together but never got noticed. She was tired of being the one who won races and got elected president, but didn't get asked to the dance. She was tired of being drab, dependable Meg McCall.

She turned to Sean, Nick's name almost on her lips. But instead she said, "Did you ride your bike?"

Sean was scratching dried paint off his hand. "Yeah. But I'll walk you home, anyway. I have to go to my locker first, though."

They slowly trampled back across the quad and into the main corridor. Suddenly exhausted, Meg plopped down on the floor while Sean spun open his locker. She stared at the mess that he had inside — bicycle helmet, pump, sweat shirt, comic books, empty lunch sacks, advanced science lab manual, and two identical copies of George Orwell's *1984*. Meg reached in and took one.

"I thought I gave this to Nick." She looked inside the cover. It was from the Redwood High Library. Due yesterday.

Sean continued to root through his locker, his movements getting a little more deliberate, almost angry. "He gave it back. He didn't even want to look at it. Too busy with. . . ."

"Football," they both said at the same time. They exchanged the briefest look, and Meg was glad she hadn't confessed her feelings to Sean. Since school had started, Nick had much less time for Sean, too, and in that moment Meg realized that Sean was also hurting. She handed the book back to him. "It's overdue."

Sean tossed it in his locker, clipped his bicycle

helmet to his belt, and slammed the door. "Oh, well." His voice did the slightest dip. A little embarrassed, he led the way toward the parking lot.

Meg followed, staring at Sean as he shuffled out, his helmet bumping against his hip, two books under each arm. They reached the parking lot and Sean bent over the bike rack. He secured his books, unlocked the chain, and began walking his bike toward the street.

"Sean, do you think you can make yourself change, if you want to?" Meg asked when she caught up with him at the corner.

They waited for the light, then slowly crossed the street.

"What do you mean?"

She paused, then decided — if she couldn't discuss this kind of thing with Sean, who could she discuss it with? "What if all of a sudden I decided I wanted to be, I don't know . . . wild, not so dependable."

Sean cracked a sad smile. "Like Madonna?"

Meg almost laughed. The vision of herself in lace underwear was too absurd. "I'm serious. Maybe I need to be different." They started toward their block and Meg put a hand on Sean's arm. "Sean, do you think guys don't like girls who are too good at everything?"

"I'm probably not the best person to ask about stuff like that," he admitted, "but I don't see why guys should like girls who mess everything up."

"I'm not so sure." Meg thought back to Whitney. Whitney had sure messed things up with Celia and Allie, and Nick seemed to like her. Of course, Whitney was beautiful and fashionable and a great flirt and all those other things that Meg McCall was not.

"Do you ever wish you could be somebody else?" Meg asked.

Sean rolled his eyes as if Meg had just made the understatement of the century. Then he hiked his bike up over the curb. "Like Bruce Springsteen?" He did a sudden guitar riff with one hand, making loud bending sounds as he pretended to strum. "How's that?"

Meg had to smile. At last that icy reserve she'd built up over the last two weeks was beginning to defrost. "Not bad. I think I'd like to be Molly Ringwald."

"Tom Cruise."

"Moon Unit Zappa," Meg giggled. "At least people would remember my name."

"Michael J. Fox." Sean shrugged. "I'm almost short enough."

They'd reached their block and Meg started for her house. Sean stayed on the opposite sidewalk. She walked backward and held her braids on top of her head. "Maybe I should do something, though — start dressing like Cyndi Lauper."

"And I'll wear my hair like Prince."

They both laughed, then stopped and gazed at each other from either side of the street. Meg sighed. She knew that Sean might change more than any of them. Sometimes she looked in his sweet eyes and saw a boy who could one day be almost as handsome as Nick. But what about her? "Sometimes I really do wish I could be anybody besides me."

"I know the feeling." Sean pulled his bike up onto his lawn. "Who knows, maybe we will change one day. I'll turn into Gumby, or E.T."

"No. Not you."

Sean suddenly looked serious. "Don't worry, Meg. You could be anything you wanted."

"You think so?"

Sean did another guitar riff. "Why not?"

He dragged his bicycle up his front steps and turned back to wave good-bye. Meg watched him, then slowly walked past Celia's house and up to her own front door. As she opened it, she couldn't help wondering if Sean was right. Maybe Meg McCall would surprise them one day after all.

Just after Meg went into her house, and Sean disappeared into his, a white BMW pulled up. It stopped right where Sean and Meg had been standing, but it didn't park. The motor continued to hum and, as it did, Celia pushed on the seat in front of her and, trying to be ladylike, climbed out.

"Wait here. I'll just run in and change."

Celia looked hopefully at Whitney and Whitney's sister Julianne. Julianne, a senior, sat behind the wheel looking even more confident, more beautiful, and better dressed than Whitney.

"Take your time," Whitney insisted.

Celia was relieved. The last thing she wanted was for either of them to come inside with her. Even though Celia knew her mother was working late, the thought of Whitney or Julianne seeing their greenish shag carpet, or the card table in the living room, or the black-and-white TV with the tinfoil balled on the antenna made Celia want to crawl in a closet and hide.

"I'll only be a minute," Celia called back as she threw open the screen door and bolted inside.

She didn't really even like Whitney and Julianne seeing the outside of her house — how it was the smallest on the block, the only one with an overgrown yard and no garage — but she had no choice. She had to change out of her cheerleading outfit before going to Nick's for dinner, and Whitney had insisted on giving her a ride.

As quickly as possible, Celia went into her room, threw her top and skirt onto the floor, and rifled through her drawers. There was a Ralph Lauren sweater that she'd found secondhand — it even had the polo player on it. She slipped that on and a pair of corduroy jeans, put a band in her hair — a dark brown plastic one she'd found at the Rexall that looked a lot like Whitney's — and reached for the light switch. But as she did, her breathing stopped. Through the other room Celia could see Whitney standing in the entrance holding open the screen door.

"I'm ready," Celia said, trying to sound casual.

Whitney didn't budge. She still had on her cheerleading outfit, and her hair was backlit by the street lamps. She looked like an angel.

"I was wondering," Whitney sighed sweetly. "Julianne says that our folks aren't home and we're supposed to go out for dinner, but you and I've been having so much fun today, and I thought we should celebrate our first game. . . ." Whitney smiled and hesitated.

102

Celia was confused. Was Whitney asking her to go out to dinner, too? But what if Whitney chose someplace fancy and expensive? What would Celia do then? Desperate to avoid that situation, Celia thought fast.

"Do you want to eat at Nick's? I could call and ask. They always have enough food for twenty people."

Whitney held the door and leaned back, swinging. She was smiling so broadly she was practically purring. "Okay," she said, her voice full of cool surprise. "Just me, though. Julianne will probably want to go to her boyfriend's."

Celia picked up the phone, trying to hide the dirty breakfast dishes that were still on the table, and called her aunt. Sure enough, Nick's mom extended her invitation to include Whitney. A moment later, Celia was leading Whitney back out the door, and they were on their way.

"I want to stop home and change, too, before we go to Nick's," Whitney ordered as they drove past Redwood High and toward the vineyards and sprawling ranches.

Julianne gave her an irritated look, then clucked her tongue. "Don't worry, Whitney. You look just fine." The sisters laughed, as if at some private joke, and then, for the first time that afternoon, Julianne looked back and acknowledged Celia. "You know, you two were the only decent-looking cheerleaders on the field. The others were pathetic."

Celia was speechless. The other cheerleaders were all older than she and Whitney, and Celia admired them. She would never dream of bad-mouthing them. She stared out the window.

Julianne continued, "That one with the short hair . . . Ann something. Somebody should tell her that those are not thighs you want to show to the world. And," she started to laugh, "if her eyes were any closer together they'd be on the other side of her face."

Whitney giggled and looked back at Celia. Not sure how to react, Celia felt herself smile.

"I know," Whitney said with a muffled voice. "But the worst is Jennifer. I swear she has a mustache."

Julianne howled. Whitney looked back at Celia. "Have you ever noticed that?"

"I guess."

"And Rebecca Steinmetz," continued Julianne. "She's okay-looking, but the way she led those yells. She has the personality of a dial tone."

Now even Celia had to laugh. It was true that beautiful Rebecca had been so nervous that she'd barely smiled through the whole game.

"But I looked okay?" Whitney checked.

Julianne turned the wheel, pulling into a long private driveway. "You looked fabulous. The only decent thing out there." Suddenly Julianne looked at Celia in the rearview mirror. She wore a funny expression, as if Whitney had just elbowed her in the ribs. "And you, too," Julianne assured Celia. "Of course, you looked great, too."

"Thank you," Celia replied.

They drove along the driveway, which was longer than most city blocks. As their colonial-style house came into view, Celia pitched forward, her mouth falling open with envy. Julianne and Whitney continued to chatter and laugh, while Celia sat in the back staring and nodding her head.

"Daddy, you're being so unfair!"

"I don't think so."

"But he's very responsible. He really is."

"I'm sure of that, Allie."

"Daddy, I'm not a baby anymore."

Allie continued to argue as she got out of the car. She crossed the garage, waiting while her father pressed the automatic opener and watched the light go out and the door swing down. That was just the way she was feeling. Everything she cared about, all the excitement she'd felt over meeting L.P., it was all going dark inside because her father was being so stubborn.

"Look, Daddy," she said, lowering her voice. "I'll invite him over and you can meet him."

Her father sighed. Under his arm was a stack of papers — exams from his students at the university — and he handed them to Allie as he opened the back door. Following him, she marched through the living room and the hall to his study. She dumped the papers on his desk, which was already stacked high with books and journals, and turned right around. "How about it?" she said.

From the way his bald spot was reddening, Allie knew that he was getting angry, but she was beginning not to care. It was so stupid! She tried to make her point.

"Celia's mom let her date over the summer, and Celia's a month younger than I am. Every other freshman I know is allowed to date."

Her father leaned over his desk. "You're not every other freshman."

"Daddy, he's not some creep. He's a nice guy."

"I'm sure he is. But you are still not allowed to drive with a boy who just got his license."

"Dad! What am I supposed to do, ask his mother to pick me up? Come on."

Mr. Simon gave her a weary look. "Allie, I know you think I'm an ogre, but I'm not being unreasonable. You can go to the dance with your friends and meet this boy there, and then come home with Celia and Meg."

"But Daddy, it's a date."

"Case closed. You can go with Meg and Celia." Her father turned around and went into the kitchen.

Allie started to follow him so she could appeal to her mother. But when she heard baby Emily let loose with a piercing scream, she knew that her mother would be too preoccupied to help. Why did her mom have to have a baby now, when Allie needed her more than ever! Allie chewed on her thumbnail and decided in that moment how she would handle the situation. *She would lie.* She'd tell her parents she was going with Celia and Meg, but really drive to the dance with L.P. She'd figure out how to make it all work, but first she had to talk to Celia and make sure that she would cover for her.

The telephone kept ringing — Celia obviously wasn't home. But why? It was way after the game had ended! Where was she? Next Allie tried Meg. Busy. In desperation to talk to someone — anyone — she tried Sean. But his phone was busy, too.

"Probably talking to each other," Allie blurted as the first tear started to spill. Where were her friends when she needed them!

The tears were now coming down like rain, and Allie was afraid her father might see. Emily was still crying in the kitchen, and her brother, Fletcher, was yelling at the TV, and it was all making her feel even crazier. Wiping her face, she left the dining room and went out into the front yard. The huge lawn stretched out in front of her, and Allie felt the way she had two years ago when she'd run away and hid in the tree house — feeling that her father was suffocating her, tying her down so that it was impossible for her to breathe.

"I can't stand it!"

Her words were answered by a whoosh of wind and the crackle of a car pulling onto the dirt road that led to Nick's driveway next door. Eventually Allie heard voices and saw Celia's blonde head just visible against the darkening dusk. Before she thought about it, she was running across her yard, through the small apple orchard, and into Nick's driveway.

"Celia!!!" she hollered.

Celia turned and stared. She started to smile, then looked a bit confused. A minute later Whitney Hain popped out of the white car next to them.

The three girls froze, staring at one another

107

until Nick's mother came out onto the porch. Mrs. Rhodes waved impatiently. "Well, come on in, kids, dinner's on the table." She spotted Allie. "You, too, Allie. There's so much food, you have to come and help eat it. I'll call your folks."

Allie looked at Celia. She didn't want to eat dinner, but it was really important that they talk. She tried to figure out how to bring it up, but before any words came, Celia was heading for the door.

"Come on, Al. Let's go in," Celia urged, with a touch of annoyance.

Allie couldn't help but notice the cold sneer on Whitney's face. She tried to catch up with Celia, but Celia had already slipped inside. With no appetite at all, Allie followed Whitney in to dinner.

CHAPTER 10

After dinner in the Rhodes kitchen, dishes were piled everywhere and the silverware had barely been rinsed, but already a water fight had broken out.

"Allie, it's your turn to be the submarine."

"No, Nick! No! Don't do that. I told you I. . . ."

Nick had Allie by the wrist and was tugging her back over to the kitchen faucet, which was running full blast. She struggled, but he secured her with one strong arm so that the more she pulled away, the tighter his hold became.

"Nick!"

"You asked for it."

He held her next to the sink full of dinner dishes and began batting water at her. Allie squinched up her eye as big droplets splatted down her cheeks. One side of her hair was soaked and there were drips trickling down the buttons on her jeans jacket.

Allie shrieked as a fan of water hit the side of her neck. *"Nicckkkkk!!!!"*

Wooof!

"Nick, cut it out. Hughie's starting to get mad."

"Shhhh!" Celia hushed.

It was no use. Nick had grabbed Allie now and was tickling her. If anything, things had gotten louder.

Celia cringed and made a fist. This evening was getting worse and worse. When they had first showed up, Nick and Allie had been so gloomy and gruff; then all through the meal Whitney and Allie had been glaring at each other as if they were on opposite sides of the Civil War; and then there was Celia, right in the middle — the Mason-Dixon line — trying to pacify both sides. Now, when she was exhausted from her peace-keeping efforts, Allie and Nick had decided to revert to their usual high spirits and have a water fight. Normally she would have been right in there splashing away, and it was *funny*, but at the same time she felt this pressure building inside her . . . the pressure not to be stupid. At least Whitney was still in the dining room, behind the French doors. She was talking politely with Nick's parents. Thank God for that.

Some stray drops of water flew toward Celia and she leaped back. "You're getting everything all wet. Come on, you guys!"

Celia's warning had the opposite effect from what she'd hoped. Nick and Allie united and turned toward her. They both looked carried away, almost possessed — as if they were getting out whatever frustrations had been bothering both of them at dinner. Even Hughie was panting and drooling like a mad thing.

"It's Celia's turn now," Nick and Allie teased. Allie put her hands up against her eyebrows as if she were some kind of monster beetle, and Nick got a weird look in his eyes and started taking big, frozen steps.

"Ha, ha, ha," Celia said sarcastically.

But it didn't stop them. Instead, they kept walking toward her, playing the same Zombie game that they used to play back in seventh grade. Celia knew how the game turned out — she'd get doused and tickled. It had been fun when they were twelve but not anymore. She backed into the doorway as they came for her, but she wasn't swift enough. They each grabbed one of her wrists hard and pulled her toward the sink and Hughie.

"NO!" Celia told them.

But they were both laughing so hard, they didn't pay any attention. Celia was starting to panic. The idea of facing Whitney with her Ralph Lauren sweater smelling like an old wet dog and her hair a mass of strawlike frizz made her want to scream.

"*Stop it!*" she yelled.

Her voice came out deep and angry, and she could tell that the tone shocked Nick and Allie. They let go of her and stepped back. Nick handed Allie a dish towel and then took one to dry his own face.

"Sorry," Nick said. He looked confused. "We were just fooling around."

"I don't care!" Celia said angrily. "It's dumb,

111

stupid. We quit doing that a long time ago."

There was an awkward silence. Celia knew she had overreacted, and she hadn't meant to yell. But she was trying her hardest to find a new Celia — a Celia who had class and sophistication, a Celia who was an equal to a girl like Whitney Hain — and indulging in silly water fights was not the way to do it.

All three of them tensed as they heard the scraping of chairs against the wooden floor and the opening of French doors from down the hall. Obviously they had been heard in the dining room. As an insistent pair of footsteps clipped toward them, Celia faced the counter and rested her head in her hands. All she needed now was to get yelled at by her aunt.

But when the kitchen door opened, Whitney was the only one standing there. She was all in white — crisply pressed slacks, blouse, and long oversize blazer. The only color on her was her rosebud mouth and the pastel bands and faces of her watches. She entered with a bright smile, but when she noticed the puddles and drips, her eyes narrowed. Finally she stared at Allie, who Celia had to admit looked as if she'd just taken a run through the sprinklers. Whitney shook her head slowly. Humiliated, Celia avoided her eyes and opened the dishwasher.

"I told your parents that we'd take care of all the cleanup," Whitney told Nick. She picked up a stack of white dessert plates and carried them over to the sink. As she handed them to Celia, Hughie barked. "Nick," Whitney said, turning back. Her voice was controlled and smoky. "Your folks are so nice."

Nick tossed his towel on the counter. Whitney was smiling at him, but he refused to respond to her compliment. His grumpiness had suddenly returned, and Celia found herself wondering how a guy who was usually so genial could suddenly act like such an ill-mannered jerk. Then, to make things even worse, Hughie picked just that moment to park himself in the middle of the floor and violently shake the water off his coat. Beads of dirty brown water went flying in every direction.

Whitney jumped back. "Eww! Make him stop!" she cried. She grabbed a dish towel and shielded herself.

Allie instantly dropped to the linoleum and put her arms around the dog. "Don't do that in here, Hughie Bear," she soothed. She looked up at Celia, but Celia looked away. Allie was now mottled with mud, but she stood and talked to Hughie again. "Let's take you outside for a walk."

Hughie perked up and trotted over to the back door. When Allie followed, Celia went back to the dishes.

Whitney started to walk over to Nick, but he was following Allie and the dog. "I'm going, too," he said. "We'll be back in a few minutes."

He clapped his hands and led Hughie out the back door and into the yard. Allie hesitated in the doorway.

"Celia," Allie said.

Celia waited before turning around. She first

took in the look on Whitney's face. Whitney was staring at Allie and her bow mouth had gone tense and knotted. Celia could see why. Allie looked even scrungier than the dog — and after hugging Hughie she probably smelled as bad, too.

"What?" Celia answered flatly.

Allie responded to Celia's cool tone by self-consciously fingering her damp hair. She looked out the window. It was dark outside, but the yard was well lit. Further off, the lights reflected on the surface of the swimming pool. "I just wanted to talk to you, that's all," Allie mumbled. "There's something important I have to ask you. It's about the dance."

Whitney stared at Allie and folded her arms over her perfectly starched chest. "Well, ask," she said, amused by Allie's awkwardness.

"Yeah, Al," Celia prodded. "What is it?"

Allie gave one voiceless, angry huff. With the briefest glance at Whitney, she tossed back her hair. "Forget it. It's private. I'll talk to you about it later." She started to go, then turned back. "That is, if you can find time to talk to me."

With that, Allie angrily slammed the door and left.

Celia waited a moment for her thoughts to clear, then tried to smile at Whitney.

"They're both in kind of weird moods tonight," Celia said.

"I guess so."

Celia began rinsing the plates and placing them in the dishwasher. Whitney came up next to her to help.

114

"Do you want an apron?" Celia asked, suddenly aware that Whitney's perfect white outfit might get soiled.

"Thanks," Whitney smiled.

Celia scurried over to the pine cabinet — which like everything else in the Rhodes house was beautiful and antique — and pulled out the prettiest apron she could find and handed it to Whitney.

"Nick's just in a bad mood because he lost his first game," Whitney suggested.

Celia knew that was partially true. When Nick had been forced to describe the game to his father over dinner, her cousin had gone a little pale. Still, Celia knew him well enough to sense that something else was weighing on him as well.

"Now, Allie," Whitney sighed. She moved closer to Celia and almost whispered. "I know she's your good friend, but she's so. . . ." Whitney couldn't find the words.

Celia figured that Whitney was too kind to tell her what she really thought of Allie, but she also knew that Allie was one of the most loyal, imaginative, fun people in the world. Why did it have to be so hard? Lately, Celia felt so torn when she was with her. Allie was suddenly all the things that Celia didn't want to be anymore — silly, awkward, uncool. She was so opposite from Whitney, and Celia didn't know how to make the two parts of her life fit together.

"We've been friends since we were little," Celia said, as if that would explain everything.

Whitney picked up the antique water goblets that weren't allowed in the dishwasher and began to dry them. "I know. But Celia, I probably shouldn't say this to you, but . . . well. . . ."

"What?"

Whitney put down her glass and towel and looked right into Celia's eyes. Her beautiful face was so serious that it almost made Celia's heart stop. "She's a loser," Whitney stated. "This is hard for me to say, but if you hang out with losers, everyone will think you're a loser, too. Julianne says it starts the first day of high school — people figure out what niche to put you in. And once you get stuck there, it can be very hard to change."

Celia shuddered. She had always been afraid of being stuck forever on that shelf beneath everybody else, where people could look down on her and make jokes at her expense. Her mother was like that — even at the salon, her mom's rich lady customers laughed at her. Her mom would make loud jokes and the ladies would giggle and whisper to each other. It was so clear to Celia that the ladies were laughing *at* her mother, never with her. Just thinking about it made Celia's stomach go tight. Still, Celia couldn't bear the thought of giving up the girl who'd been her best friend forever.

"I know Allie's kind of immature, but when you get to know her, she's funny and really nice. She has this laugh that makes everybody else laugh, too."

"I've heard it," Whitney came back icily. Her eyes were like cold steel.

"She's not so bad," Celia almost pleaded.

"She's a loser." Suddenly Whitney laughed.

"Did you see all the buttons she had on her jeans jacket? She looks like a bulletin board."

Celia felt that awful smile creep onto her face again — like when she'd been in the car and Whitney and Julianne had made fun of the other cheerleaders. She was so taken aback when Whitney or her sister came up with those clever put-downs. Much as Celia knew the put-downs were nasty and mean, she couldn't help laughing and wishing that she'd thought of them first. "Well, she's been collecting them since she was twelve."

"I believe it. She should get one that says, 'Honk if You Love Losers.'"

Celia heard a giggle come out of her own throat, and suddenly she wanted to one-up Whitney, to come back with something so witty and superior that everyone would have to laugh with her — not at her. "How about 'Save the Simps'?" Celia giggled.

Whitney laughed harder and looked at Celia with new respect. "That's great." She patted Celia's arm and chuckled some more. "She's still so lame, I can't imagine what she was like in middle school."

Celia couldn't stop herself. She was basking in Whitney's approval and the words just poured out. "She can be so dumb! This one time she wore a bra under her bathing suit at this swim party of Nick's. She didn't even know you weren't supposed to."

"You're kidding!"

"No, I swear."

Whitney was doubled over with glee. "Oh, no!!"

"Really!"

"Oh, gross. That is so gross!"

They laughed some more, both bending over chuckling and stamping their feet. But when Celia stood back up she spotted Allie out the back window and their laughter started to sound ugly. Allie was playing catch with Hughie, lobbing him the ball, running after him, and throwing her arms around his neck with generosity and affection. She looked totally innocent and loving. Celia turned back to the sink and began furiously finishing the dishes. She suddenly felt so dirty that every crumb annoyed her.

Whitney was just catching her breath. "You are really something, Celia, you know that. Julianne said it the first time she saw you — that you were somebody worth being friends with. And she was right."

Celia put her head down, unable to look out the window anymore. "Gee, thanks, Whitney," she managed. She turned the water on harder and began to scrub.

CHAPTER 11

"Come on, Hugh. It's okay. I won't tell."

The den was deserted and the door closed. Nick patted the love seat, assuring Hughie that it was all right to climb up next to him, even though Hughie clearly knew that lying on the furniture, especially when he was so wet and muddy, was definitely not allowed. But when Nick patted the seat again, Hughie leaped up and his tail thump-thumped against the pillows.

"Thatta boy. Yeah."

Nick tried to get comfortable as Hughie stretched out over his lap, but the back of his polo shirt was still wet from the water fight and his whole left side was starting to hurt from the game.

"What's going on, Hugh? Why is everybody acting so weird?"

Nick petted Hughie's head as the dog whined

softly. What was happening to his old friends? Nick wondered. Since school had started they'd all been acting stranger and stranger. Nick had always taken his friends for granted. They had always been there for him, and he'd always known what he should give in return. But lately with Meg, Allie, and Sean he felt as if they were communicating from two distant hilltops. By the time the messages reached each other, they were garbled and all mixed up.

Meg's coldness hit Nick the hardest of all. He didn't know why she was suddenly so angry at him. He'd gone over it again and again in his head. It seemed to have started that day they raced in gym class. But nothing had happened that day. Or had it? When Nick thought back to the race, he felt even more confused. Maybe she was angry because he wasn't helping with the Haunted House. Or maybe she just didn't like him anymore.

That was a painful thought, and Nick pushed it out of his head as fast as he could. He missed Meg — her ease and grace, that clarity in her blue eyes that reminded him of the sky in spring. He missed the jokes that they could tell together — the ones where he knew only the beginning and she the end. He missed that I-dare-you look on her face that made him do things he didn't know he could do. He missed her smile and her lanky walk and that happy, safe feeling he had when he was with her. He missed. . . .

"Girls," Nick muttered, pushing Meg's face out of his mind. There was something else he missed, but he couldn't put it in words, because he didn't quite understand what it was. All he knew was that girls were crazy and unpredictable. Celia had been so uptight lately. She reacted to that dumb water fight as if they were trying to nuke the kitchen. And Allie . . . finally she'd been her goofy, normal self, then, two minutes later, when they were out in the backyard, she was crying her eyes out but insisting that nothing was the matter!

Then there was Whitney. "Whew," Nick heaved a hugh sigh. He had no idea what Whitney wanted from him . . . no idea. He had started out being nice to her for the sake of his father, but what was he supposed to do when she pressed up against him the way she did today after the game? She was great-looking and all that, but she also could make him awfully nervous. Too nervous, in fact.

Nick sat up. "I wish Sean was here," he told Hughie, but then Sean was getting to be as much of a problem as the girls. Why did Sean have to act like that at the Haunted House today — drumming those cans and wearing that stupid cap on his head? Why did Sean do things like that? It just gave those guys an excuse to laugh at him.

Nick picked up a pillow and pitched it angrily at the windowseat. Sean had to understand that these guys were jocks. He wished he could say, Sean, these guys are just ragging you. They may give you junk but there's no harm in it; in fact, sometimes it's even a way of being friends. And guys, this is Sean. He can outlast me on a bike or a hiking trip. He can launch model rockets from a tree house and predict exactly where they'll land. He can pull fantastic pranks, like the time he and I sabotaged our swimming pool and it turned into a giant pond of soap bubbles.

Nick smiled thinking about Sean and their times together. It would be great right now to climb back up to the old tree house with Sean and listen to the apples go *thunk!* hitting the ground . . . bring up some firecrackers to toss or attach to balsa wood gliders. They could take Hughie with them and put the hatch down so none of the girls could join them. And Nick wouldn't worry about football; he wouldn't worry about girls; he wouldn't worry about social games, or who was mad at who, or if you were a jock or a brain or nerd or a preppie or a sosh.

But Nick knew it was impossible to go back, not after everything that had happened in the last few weeks. And the more he thought about it the emptier he felt.

Nick laid his cheek against the top of Hughie's soft head and whispered, "Thank God for you, Hugh. You're the only one I can count on anymore."

But Nick was going to need more than Hughie to protect him. Whitney didn't care much who Nick counted on, or where he wanted to be. All she cared about was finding him.

She walked through the living room, stopping for an instant in front of a mirror to see how she looked. The steam from the sink had made her hair extra full and little ringlets formed around her face, but she couldn't quite decide if she liked it. Maybe okay — her skin did look very rosy and there wasn't a sign of you-know-what. If the slightest bump had been evident, Whitney might have lost her nerve.

But not now. The way she looked now everything was just right, and she knew this was her big chance. Celia was on the sun porch chatting with her aunt and uncle, and Allie was still moping in the backyard. Whitney had seen Nick come in, and by all logical deduction he should be alone. But the trick was to find him. The whole point of manipulating her way into dinner tonight was to have some time alone with Nick, and now that she was here, nothing was going to get in her way.

Whitney turned and continued down the hall. She slowed for a moment to look at a framed collection of photographs, a collage of family snapshots from years gone by. She could see that even as a little boy Nick had been handsome. His hair had been even lighter — like Celia's was now, instead of that dark gold. Julianne was right; he was the only boy who had everything: looks, manners, money, status, family, and popularity. . . .

But Julianne had also warned her when she'd heard about Nick's childhood friends — get rid of them, her sister had said. Split them up, now and for good, otherwise they will pull you and Nick down and it won't be worth it. So Whitney was doing just that.

Celia was all right — she was Nick's cousin and a beauty — although Whitney couldn't figure out how one branch of the family had ended up with everything while the other side only got looks. And there was such a thing, Whitney was beginning to believe, as being too pretty. Too pretty without the right clothes and background was like being too hungry when you went to a fine restaurant. The prettiness was ruined by going after everything too blindly, too desperately, too fast. Still, Whitney needed Celia, and so Celia would remain.

But the others? Meg McCall wasn't really worth bothering about with her don't-notice-me clothes and the way she worked, worked, worked. Even though she was popular and could have been good-looking if she tried, she was too nice . . . one of those girls who'd fall to the wayside on her own. But Allie Simon? *Allie Simon???* She was one big Fashion Don't — like those pictures of girls with the X's across them in *Glamour*. Then there was that little wimp, Sean. With that squeaky voice and scrawny body, he was like a reject from elementary school. . . . How Nick wasn't embarrassed just to know him was beyond Whitney's comprehension.

Whitney checked her three watches and continued down the hall. Julianne was coming for her soon so she had to hurry. She went for the next door and pushed it open. As she did a gasp came up from her throat and her heart started to flutter like a hummingbird. She'd finally found him. Nick was sitting on a small sofa, staring blankly out the window into the side yard. And, except for the dog, he was all alone.

"Hi," Whitney said, trying to sound surprised.

Nick looked up. His green eyes were slightly glazed, watery. "Hi."

Whitney walked slowly his way. She had gone over this moment so many times with Julianne. Don't bother talking, her sister had told her. Do it with your body. Sit close to him, look into his face until he has to kiss you.

Whitney had been practicing that afternoon at the game when she put her arms around Nick's neck. She'd sensed then that he liked her, and it had given her confidence.

"What are you doing?"

Nick looked down. "Nothing much."

Whitney was trying to figure out a way to sit next to Nick. Julianne had stressed that — sitting close to him on a couch or the arm of a big chair. But the love seat — which would have been perfect for her and Nick — was half-filled up by a hairy, smelly dog. That's one more thing that has to go from Nick's life, Whitney thought.

She took a few steps closer and Hughie growled.

"Hey, what's that?" Nick wondered. He stood up, and Hughie sprang down onto the floor. "Come on, Hugh, you'd better get out of here before Mom catches you." Hughie didn't budge until Nick picked up a *Gourmet* magazine from the side table and whacked it against his hand. "Go on, get out of here." Hughie barked and trotted off down the hall.

Whitney watched Nick sit back down. He looked so preoccupied tonight, so sad. She liked the way his legs were almost too long for the old sofa and how his polo shirt was tucked so neatly inside the waistband of his jeans. She slowly walked over and perched on the very edge of the love seat. As she did, Nick eased over to give her more room.

"Are you still upset about the game?"

Nick shrugged. "Not really."

Whitney brushed a few dogs hairs off her white slacks. Nick was sitting forward, his elbows on his knees and hands clasped. He was barely looking at her. Whitney had a sudden moment of doubt. She found herself wondering if this wasn't another of Julianne's great schemes to make somebody else look like a fool.

"You really were great," Whitney said as sweetly as she could. When he didn't react, she decided to change her tactics. "Don't worry, Nick. It's only the first one. There's a lot of games left."

Finally Nick raised his head and almost smiled. "I know. Did you have a good time? You and Celia looked great out there."

"Really? You noticed us?"

"All the guys did."

"Really! We tried to cheer you on, but I guess we didn't do a very good job."

"It wasn't your fault."

Whitney inched over just as Nick looked at her, and in that moment, she knew that Julianne's advice had been right. When she caught his eye, he seemed unable to look away. She tilted her face up to his and pressed her shoulder closer, then everything seemed to go into slow motion, as if her whole body were made of liquid. Whitney let her neck fall back, never taking her eyes off

126

Nick's. And he began to move very slowly toward her. First his hand touched her shoulder and then his eyes began to close. . . .

Then there was a loud gasp, and Nick jumped back.

"OOPS! Sorry."

The door to the den had flown all the way open and Allie, her hair still a mess from the water fight, her eyes red and puffy, was standing in the doorway looking confused.

"Um, I was looking for Celia. I have to talk to her."

Allie froze as she stared at the two of them, but by this time Nick had popped up and was already skirting past her into the hall.

"I don't know where she is," he grumbled. "I'll go look for her." A moment later, he was gone.

Whitney rose from the love seat. She glared at Allie with the full force of her powerful, cold eyes.

Allie's shoulders slumped forward and she turned to go.

"Allie," Whitney ordered, stopping her.

Allie halted. She couldn't meet Whitney's eyes and stood awkwardly in the doorway. "Huh?"

"I want to tell you something."

"What?"

Whitney moved up close to her and spoke in a low voice. "I think you should know that you need to make some new friends. Nick and Celia have outgrown you."

"What?"

"They don't want to hang out with you anymore. It's so obvious."

Allie was stunned. "Maybe you're the one that needs some other friends." She fought back blindly. "What makes you think they like you so much? It looked to me like Nick couldn't wait to get away from you."

Rage burned through Whitney. How dare this wimp, this reject, say something like that to her! "You are such an embarrassment to them," Whitney spat out cruelly. "Anybody who wears a bra under her bathing suit at a swimming party. I'm sure they both loved that!"

Allie looked up from the floor for the first time. Her face was white and she was unable to speak. Her hands started to tremble, and the tears filled her eyes before she could even think about trying to hold them back.

Whitney laughed. She mimed pulling a bra strap up from her shoulder. " 'Bye," she whispered, and with a triumphant smile, she stomped out.

Allie's shoulders were shaking and the tears were pouring down, and her chest was heaving like a bellows. Celia wouldn't have told . . . she couldn't have told . . . her best friend forever and . . . but who else could have told Whitney her secret? Nick? Never. Meg or Sean? Impossible. It had to be Celia. How else —

A loud wail escaped from Allie's throat and she tried to quiet herself. All she needed now was for Celia and Whitney to find her sobbing like a five-year-old. Barely able to see, she tore down the hall toward the back door. Past the living room, the dining room, the sun porch . . . finally she reached the kitchen and went into the backyard. She would run back through the orchard, and sneak home into her room, where she would hide forever, never speaking to anyone ever again.

But before she made it to the apple trees Celia's voice stopped her.

"Allie! Allie, wait!"

Allie looked back and saw Celia, and farther off the swimming pool, an old wrought-iron table, the brick barbecue, Nick's mom's flower garden, and the tree house. But her vision was so blurred that she couldn't tell where one stopped and the others began.

Celia was running up to her. "Are you going home already? I thought you wanted to talk to me about something." When she got closer and saw Allie's face, she reached out her hand. Allie backed away. "Al, what is it? What happened?"

Allie started crying again, and Celia stepped forward to put her arms around her. But this time Allie rejected her so violently that Celia looked almost as hurt as she. "Allie," Celia begged, "please tell me what's wrong."

Allie shook her head and continued to weep.

"Al! Talk to me. Please!"

Finally Allie caught her breath long enough to speak. She raised her head. "I don't ever want to talk to you again as long as I live."

They stood there for one more painful second before Allie took off through the orchard and ran home.

CHAPTER 12

Allie kept her word.

At first Celia'd called, but Allie hung up. Celia'd approached Allie in the halls at school, but Allie pretended she didn't see her and kept on walking. Celia'd even sent notes, but Allie tore them into little pieces. After fifteen agonizing days, Allie had succeeded in not communicating at all with her ex-best friend — not a sentence, not a syllable, not even a sullen gesture or hello.

Of course, that didn't stop Allie from being curious about Celia. She wondered constantly what Celia was doing, and what, if anything, Celia had said about her.

"So Celia's going to the dance, too?" Allie breathlessly asked Meg. The evening of Redwood High's first dance had finally arrived and Allie and Meg sat on Meg's bed — Allie all dressed up, Meg still in her slip. Allie was kneeling behind

Meg, rolling Meg's long hair in spiky electric curlers.

"She said she was."

"Did she say what time she was going tonight? I don't want to run into her."

"She'll probably get there around eight, like the rest of us." Meg flinched. "Ow. That one hurts, Al."

"Oops." Allie uncurled the roller and wrapped it again. "So is she going with Whitney, or does she have a date?"

"She doesn't have a date. She said she wanted to dance with lots of different guys."

"That figures," Allie scoffed. "Does she know that I'm going with L.P.?"

Meg turned abruptly, causing the last curler to roll down and clunk on the floor. "Allie, why don't you call her up and ask her yourself?" Since Meg had told Celia exactly why Allie was so mad at her, both Allie and Celia had been bombarding her with questions. Meg was getting tired of being their message service.

Allie looked hurt. "Sorry."

"That's okay." Meg picked up the roller and handed it back. She knew that Allie was nervous, and she didn't want to make things worse, but all Allie could talk about lately was Celia and Whitney and L.P. Considering that Meg was about to go to her first high school dance, too, she had a few other things on her mind.

Meg flicked on her cassette player and Cyndi Lauper's voice came out of the small tinny speaker. Meg needed something to bolster her confidence. Next to her bed, surrounded by plants,

131

pottery, stacks of books, and an old wooden rocking horse, was a mountain of discarded clothes. Usually Meg grabbed the first thing she saw in her closet — the main criterion being whether or not it was clean — but tonight she'd decided no sweat shirts and Levis, no tomboyish overalls and farm-girl braids. Still, putting together something more alluring out of her plain wardrobe wasn't easy. Allie had brought some things for her, but Meg wasn't sure she could go to a dance in somebody else's clothes.

"When is L.P. coming?" Meg asked over the music. She stared at herself in the mirror. Already Allie'd put green shadow over Meg's eyes, a touch of blush, mascara, and pinkish lipstick. Allie'd assured Meg she knew just what to do, but as Meg looked at Allie's bright pink sweater, print miniskirt, electric blue tights, and ten-plus bracelets, she wondered if Allie was the person she really wanted in charge of this transformation.

"He said he'd pick me up at seven forty-five."

"Did you tell him that you're not supposed to be driving with him?"

"No! I just said to pick me up here because I wanted to help get ready. I guess I'll have him drop me off afterward a couple blocks from my house. My dad still thinks I'm going with you and Celia." Allie rolled her eyes at the mention of Celia's name. "As if I ever wanted to go anywhere with Celia."

Meg got up from the bed and began to pace. "What if your dad finds out?"

Allie raised both hands and her bracelets clattered. "He won't. Nothing could wreck this night." She sighed. "It's just going to be me and L.P."

Meg thought of reminding Allie that there were going to be a lot of other people at the dance, like herself for one! But when Allie got like this, there was no distracting her. Besides, Meg was glad Allie was there, even if she was preoccupied. Meg's parents were working late at the nursery. She was going to walk to the dance with Sean, but he was still out riding his bike, and considering how important this evening might be, Meg couldn't have stood facing it alone.

Meg had decided that this was the evening when Nick was going to notice her — notice her as something more than a jogging partner or an invisible childhood friend. She'd barely talked to him for weeks, hoping that she could wipe the old Meg out of his mind so that when he saw the new Meg tonight, he'd be astonished and swept away. Of course, Allie didn't know that was the reason that Meg wanted to look so different. Meg hadn't told anyone about her feelings for Nick. Not anyone.

"I guess it's time for me to get dressed, Al."

Finally Allie looked at her. Her eyes gleamed with expectation. "I'm so busy thinking about myself, I almost forget about you." Allie gave an apologetic smile and began rifling through the pile of clothes she'd brought with her. She rubbed her hands together. "Okay. We're going to make you look flashy, so every guy will fall over when he sees you."

"Nothing too radical." Meg blushed. "I just want to look different, Al. I'm just tired of being

133

— I don't know — the same old boring me."

Allie grinned. "Have no fear." She picked up a red knit dress with a vee neck that looked like a long sweater. Meg'd seen it a few times on Allie. It was actually fairly simple, and Meg breathed a sigh of relief as Allie maneuvered the wide neckline over Meg's curlers. "Remember this? My grandmother got it for me at the Esprit Outlet in San Francisco. It's one of those one-size-fits-all, so I figured you could wear it."

Meg let the dress slide down over her hips and stared in the mirror. Because she was so much taller than Allie, she'd wondered how they would ever share clothes, but this dress seemed to be okay. "It's kind of short, isn't it?"

Allie giggled and dug in the pile again. "It's going to get shorter. You have such great legs." She pulled out a wide belt that looked like it was covered in zebra fur. Before Meg could protest, Allie tied the belt around her waist and pulled the dress up so it bloused over it. Now the hemline was up to the middle of Meg's thigh. Meg tugged it down. "You look terrific," Allie squealed. "But the best is yet to come." Meg sat back down on the bed in shock as Allie pulled out a pair of white lace gloves, a necklace of plastic hearts, a trio of red and green bracelets, and a pair of red high heels. "These are my mom's," Allie said, pointing at the shoes. "She wears your size."

Allie fiddled with the accessories while Meg sat like a child getting bandaged after a bicycle accident. After Allie'd clasped and tinkered, she removed the rollers from Meg's hair till it bounced in tight curls down to the middle of her back. Meg immediately raised a hand to pat it down — suddenly her head looked so huge — but Allie pushed her hand away. "Just shake your head out and leave it."

Meg stared at herself and stood up. Her hair seemed so dark and glossy against the red, and the shoes made her feel twenty feet tall. Her eyes looked huge from the mascara, and everything about her face looked older, more defined, and feminine. The clingy dress made her look as if she had a figure, long-legged and slender, instead of just a set of straight limbs and a torso. Meg attempted a flirtatious smile in the mirror, but when she realized that Allie was watching her, she blushed and turned away.

"Do you like it?" Allie asked hopefully. "I think you look wonderful. And you sure look different."

Meg looked at herself one more time. A delicious airy excitement had just started to inflate her insides. "I do, don't I?"

Allie nodded and turned up the music full blast. They both laughed and started to dance.

Five blocks away a mint condition '65 Mustang, glossy with a recent wax job and perfect paint, was parked in the middle of the street. Two boys, brothers, both with short hair and wiry builds, sat in the front seat leaning toward each other as if they were planning a mugging.

"Don't crash it, L.P."

"It's only five more blocks. Don't worry."

"Just be careful, that's all. Dad'll kill me if he finds out I let you drive alone."

"I'm a good driver, Jed. It'll be fine."

"Just don't crash it."

L.P. waited for his older brother to step out onto the curb before sliding into the driver's seat. As he put his hands on the wheel, his throat went dry and his palms got damp. This car was his father's pride and joy; even Jed, who was nineteen, had to promise and plead to drive it. As L.P. settled into the bucket seat, he breathed in that old leather smell and touched the little horse in the middle of the steering wheel. Suddenly he understood why his dad loved this car so much.

Jed leaned in on the window frame. "I'm telling you, this makes me nervous, L.P. Why don't you just let me drive the whole time?"

"No," L.P. asserted quickly. He reached for the clutch and practiced pushing it in as he changed from gear to gear. Jed was probably right. Since L.P. was only fifteen and a half years old, and had only a learner's permit but no license, driving even five blocks without an older driver in the car was against the law. But what could L.P. do? He'd told Allie that he was going to pick her up — the two of them alone, a date. So how could he suddenly show up and explain that he really wasn't sixteen and that was why his brother had to be in the car with them? Cringing, L.P. cleared his throat.

"I'll pick you up in a few minutes," he reminded Jed. "She's at her friend's house so I won't have to meet her parents or anything. I'll just pretend that you're walking along, and I happen to see you and offer you a ride."

"You're too kind," Jed teased sarcastically.

L.P. turned the key. For a moment he couldn't coordinate the clutch and the ignition, and the gears ground with a shrill roar. His brother put his hands over his face.

"I can't watch," Jed said.

"Don't worry." L.P. carefully put the car in gear and glanced back at his brother in the side-view mirror. "Thanks. I won't forget this."

"You bet you won't," Jed called as L.P. pulled away from the curb. "I won't let you."

L.P. pulled into the street. He was hovering over the steering wheel, which felt as big as a Hula-Hoop. He drove very slowly, trying to keep his eyes peeled every second for dogs, children, bicycles, cars pulling out of driveways, motorcycles. It was awe inspiring when you really thought about the variety of things it was possible to hit in just five blocks. He slammed on the brakes when a kid on a skateboard jumped off the sidewalk and glided across the road, but he forgot the clutch and the Mustang shuddered to a halt.

"Great." L.P. swore. He checked his face in the rearview mirror. He was already sweating and wiped his forehead with the sleeve of his jacket.

He could hardly believe that he was doing this, but after that first time he'd met Allie and she'd mistaken him for a freshman, he had to do something to prove himself. As he restarted the car and tried desperately not to stall at every corner, he wondered if he was only going to do something else to give himself away. Maybe drive up over the curb or close the door on her dress or put the car in reverse when he wanted to go forward. It could easily be as bad as the first time he'd met her, when he'd dropped his umbrella and knocked over his photography light. That's all he needed — to act like a clumsy geek again.

The weird thing was, there was something about Allie that seemed kind of goofy and young, too — it was a silly look in her eyes, that crazy laugh, those wild clothes and bracelets that sounded like castanets. That was actually what he liked about her, that and the way she'd almost cried when she looked at the Georgia O'Keeffe painting on the cover of his new art book. That was what made him ask her to the dance. But he figured there was also that side of Allie that probably wanted what every other girl at Redwood High wanted — a sophisticated older guy with wheels and a cool exterior.

L.P. reached the McCall house, checking the number twice before pulling over. It was half dark, but he could see that the plants were so neat and lush he could have been in a park except for the porch lined with pottery and the car port to one side. The rest of the block was quiet except for a skinny redheaded guy across the street who was humming a rock 'n' roll riff and pushing his mountain bike into his garage. L.P. managed to park the car and got out.

As he walked up to the front door, he thought about all the awful things that could happen on this night. He could be arrested for driving without a license, he could crash his father's car and have to sell all his camera equipment to pay for the repair, he could trip Allie when they were dancing and break her leg. . . .

L.P. reached the door and took a deep breath. He rang and waited as the footsteps got closer and closer. At last the door opened and Allie stood in front of him.

"Hi."

"Hi."

"You ready?"

"Sure."

She smiled. Her face looked radiant and there was a glow in her eyes that warmed him from his toes to the top of his spiky hair. All at once he knew that nothing could possibly go wrong. And he knew that whatever he'd had to go through to make this night happen, it was all going to be worth it.

CHAPTER 13

"Did you see Mary Beth Raft? Didn't anybody ever tell her that sideways stripes and size fourteen hips are not the best combination for your first high school dance?"

"What about that plaid skirt and blazer on Madeline Edmonds? Maybe she thinks she's at St. Mary's."

"How about that low-cut dress that Karen Nudleman's wearing? I bet she's praying that guys won't look at her face!"

Celia stepped off the dance floor in time to overhear Whitney, along with Ann and Rebecca, the two sophomore cheerleaders, squeal with laughter. When Celia'd left them two songs earlier to dance with a boy in her Spanish class, Whitney was leading them in sizing up the other girls at the dance. Now Ann and Rebecca were trying to top her. Although chubby Ann was usually brassy and loud, such witticisms were unusual for lovely, composed Rebecca.

Whitney pointed. "What do you think of Jackie Peterson's hat? She looks like she forgot her broomstick and that mangy little dog, too!" Leading the others, Whitney hummed the Wicked Witch of the West music from *The Wizard of Oz* and stared at Jackie Peterson — who had made the unfortunate decision to wear a wide-brimmed black hat. Jackie couldn't ignore it for long. The humming got louder and louder until Jackie finally slunk away to the bathroom.

"Oh, poor baby," Ann sang and laughed again.

Whitney leaned toward her. "If you could only dance with one guy here, who would you pick?"

Without hesitation, Ann puckered her mouth and pointed across the cafeteria at the group of football players huddled in the opposite corner. "Terry Warner," she purred. "Hey, Becky, what about you?"

Rebecca placidly looked over the whole cafeteria. She took a long time, since the place was packed. But she ended up staring at the football jocks, too. "I'm not sure. But I wouldn't mind dancing with Mark Coffield," she said.

"Who would?" giggled Ann.

All the girls, including Celia, who'd not made a sound up to this point, nodded and ooohed. They continued to stare at the huddle, which included Mark, Terry, Jay Creary, Nick, and about five others.

"What about you, Whitney?" Celia asked. "Who would you like to dance with?"

Whitney, who was in a pale lavender dress so

airy it almost floated, answered with a coy smile. "Oh, I don't know."

They all laughed, and for an instant Celia was worried that she'd said the wrong thing.

"Well, you'd think they could all forget about football for five minutes and dance," complained Ann. She took a step out and waved, but was unsuccessful in attracting Terry's attention.

"They're probably still trying to figure out what they did wrong at yesterday's game," Rebecca added, rolling her eyes. "I sure hope they win at least one game soon. Three losses and no wins is pretty pathetic."

"Tell me about it," agreed Ann. "I'm running out of ideas for coming-from-behind cheers." She readjusted her clingy sweater and looked over at the guys again. The band — a local group called The Mighty Jungle — had just returned from its break and was getting ready for its second set. "I don't know about you guys, but I'm not standing around anymore. I'm going over and asking Terry to dance myself."

The other girls looked at her with admiration. But as soon as Ann worked up the nerve and started to leave, the huddle broke up and some of the boys headed toward them. Mark Coffield was waylaid by a pretty junior, but Terry, Jay, Nick, and a few others kept on coming. The girls got very quiet.

Nick was the first to approach. He smiled at them all, but sidled up beside Celia. She had to admit that in his jeans and navy crewneck sweater he looked even more handsome than usual.

"Hi, everybody."

Whitney gave a flirtatious smile, but he was gazing beyond her, as if he were looking for someone. Before she could approach Nick, one of the other boys asked her to dance. Looking slightly annoyed, she followed him out onto the dance floor.

"So what's going on?" Jay asked loudly. The girls gave him plenty of room. Big and noisy, he was the one guy they clearly did not want to dance with. Terry stood next to him wearing a new letterman's jacket. He stuck his hands in his pockets, rocked back and forth on his heels, and surveyed the crowd.

Finally Nick pulled Celia a few feet away. The band started to play, and he leaned toward her ear in order to be heard. "Having a good time?"

"Great." She'd barely sat out one dance during the first set.

Nick bumped her with his elbow. "All these guys keep asking you to dance. I should tell them how you used to have to wear that head brace thing for your teeth that made you look like an alien."

Celia smiled at Randall Stuart, a boy she'd danced with earlier. "You wouldn't dare."

"Nah." He moved slightly to the music. After a moment, he asked, "Have you seen Meg?"

Celia had seen Meg earlier, when Meg had arrived with Sean, and her friend had looked very un-Meglike. The clothes Meg wore were so obviously Allie's . . . and anything that reminded her of Allie made her feel very sad and mixed up.

"Not since I first got here," she answered. "But I think a bunch of freshmen are outside in the quad."

"How about Sean?"

"Maybe he's out there, too."

They both turned their attention to the music again, bobbing and rocking to the beat. They stood quietly as the band finished one song and started another.

"Is Allie here?" Celia suddenly heard herself ask. "I haven't seen her yet."

Nick shook his head. "Me, neither."

Celia was about to suggest to Nick that they go out and look for the others. Instead, she shook her head, as if she could wipe away thoughts of Allie the way you erase drawings on an Etch-a-Sketch. She reminded herself that she was having a brilliant first dance — she had danced more than almost any girl there — she was a cheer-leader, a beauty, the envy of many a freshman girl.

As if to prove it, Terry interrupted with a purposeful smile. "Hey, Celia, wanna dance?"

"Sure."

Celia followed Terry onto the floor, nudging her way between the arms and feet and hips. It was only when she looked back at Nick that she noticed a slight sneer on Ann's face.

Celia hit the center of the floor and tried to lose herself in the music. But her joy was forced. It wasn't Ann liking Terry that bothered her. It wasn't Meg or Sean or the losing football team or Whitney. It was still Allie. The orange and yellow streamers overhead reminded her of Allie's twelfth birthday party. The red and yellow paper leaves underfoot made her think of the tree house. The murals of grapes and horns-of-plenty that decorated the walls reminded her of a collage she and Allie had made together in the sixth grade.

She tried to concentrate on Terry and the music. She threw herself into her dancing as if she could expel thoughts of Allie and her own cruelty like some kind of bad spirit. This was a night she'd remember forever, she told herself.

Celia put her head back and really let herself go to the music. Her body was strong and well toned from cheerleading, and she felt so pent up inside that she wanted to leap up to the ceiling and swing on the crepe paper streamers like Tarzan. She smiled at Terry and he smiled back. She noticed that people were watching her. She continued to push the vision of Allie from her mind, hoping that the picture of a new, invincible Celia would take its place.

Meg had been outside for almost an hour. It was a lovely fall night, not too cold, with a clear, dark sky, and millions of stars, but it was obvious that she and the other freshmen who lingered in the quad were not staying out to enjoy the night air. The girls were all clearly frightened of returning to the cafeteria and not being asked to dance, while the guys were gathering up their nerve and hoping that when they finally asked a girl they wouldn't be turned down.

"Hey, Meg. Anybody home?"

It was Sean. He was sitting on a rock behind

145

her, picking blades of grass. They were surrounded by six or seven freshmen from the fundraising committee, and Meg wondered how long she'd been spacing out. Suddenly she couldn't bear sitting out there anymore. This was ridiculous. She'd never been a chicken before. Just because she was in high school was no reason for her to start being one now. She got up, hobbling a little in Allie's mother's shoes, and with great purpose headed for the cafeteria.

Sean trotted to catch up to her. "What's the matter?" he demanded, pulling up his baggy slacks. He was wearing some sort of cowboy shirt that made him look even skinnier than usual.

"Why should anything be the matter?" Meg answered as she stomped across the quad. The spike heels sank into the new grass with each step, and there was already a searing blister on her heel. "I'm just going to the dance. That's what we came here for, isn't it? Not to sit out here like lumps."

Sean shrugged and reluctantly followed. He had no real desire to go in that cafeteria again. He'd only come to keep Meg company and because his parents expected him to. His mom and dad thought he was not only a genius, but a charmer who had a million friends. They believed in him so totally that Sean couldn't bear to disappoint them. He was glad they hadn't seen him inside the cafeteria earlier when that stupid jock Jay Creary had walked by and murmured that Sean was a pathetic wimp. Sean had muttered back that Jay reminded him of Miss Piggy.

And Jay answered with a look that said, Don't even try it. Sean did not want to go back. Still, for Meg's sake, he followed.

Meg reached the entrance and gave a tight smile as she passed one of the faculty chaperons. Sean went in, but once inside, retreated to the bench in a dark corner near the door.

The music was so loud that it made Meg's head pound, and there were so many people that she couldn't quite recognize anyone. She finally spotted Celia on the dance floor. Celia was dancing with Roy somebody, who ran cross-country. She danced fervently, almost wildly. The song ended, but before Celia could get off the floor, Terry Warner rushed up to her, obviously asking her for the next dance. But the band didn't start playing right away. The girl singer, who had boyish blonde hair and wore a sparkly strapless dress, approached the mike first.

"Is everybody having a good time?"

The crowd answered with a happy roar. Meg almost put her hands over her ears. The singer leaned into the mike again. "This one is for you ladies," she said in a low, sexy voice. "It's a slow one. And it's girls' choice." She gave a knowing smile as a murmur went through the crowd, then turned back to her band as they took a moment to retune.

Meg knew this was her chance. She looked desperately for Nick. He was standing a few feet away from the cheerleader-football crowd, almost as if he wanted to be alone but didn't have the nerve to really go off by himself. There was a light just over his head that rotated, alternately painting the side of his hair the softest blues and purples. As Meg walked over to him, her ankles felt like rubber.

He looked up and when he saw her the most wonderful thing happened. His mouth curved in happy surprise and he inched over, making a space a few feet from the others for Meg to stand next to him — a little pocket of warmth and stillness in that enormous, busy room.

"Meg!"

"Hi."

"Hi. I was looking for you."

"You were?" Meg's heart beat faster.

"I didn't know if you were here or not."

"Oh."

"I guess I never found out for sure if you were coming."

"I guess not."

"Anyway, I'm glad you're here." He cleared his throat. "I kind of miss you these days."

"Me, too."

A mellow saxophone crooned. The slow song had started. Meg tried to work up her nerve to ask him to dance.

Nick turned and looked into her face. Just then the overhead light washed over Meg and the clothes that Allie had chosen for her. Nick took a step back and looked confuused.

"You look sort of, uh. . . ." He stopped. Meg could tell he wasn't sure what to say next, but she knew by the expression on Nick's face that he thought she looked ridiculous. Her heart sank like a rock. She tried to laugh, but she could tell that Nick had already noticed her reaction and was embarrassed.

"I mean, you look weird. . . ." After a moment, his face brightened. "I know what it is, you kind of look like Allie!"

Meg tried not to show it, but she could feel her throat beginning to tighten. She had so much wanted to be a different person, but not Allie. Allie was fine for Allie, but Meg wanted to be noticed as herself.

Nick clearly realized he'd said the wrong thing, but Meg could also tell he wasn't sure how to correct it. "It's not that you look bad or anything," he tried. "You just, I don't know, you don't look like you. . . ."

Meg wanted to scream, That's the whole point! I didn't want to be me tonight. I wanted to be somebody that you'd notice and ask to dance. I wanted you to forget the Meg who you think of as a sister, a dependable leader! But now it all seemed absurd. Here she was feeling nervous and shy and crazy around Nick, and avoiding him and not even having the kind of friendship with him that they used to have. And what was there instead . . . missing him all the time, and having him tell her she looked weird.

Meg was just about to say, Hey, let's forget this whole thing. Let's all five of us be together again. Let's look for raccoons with Hughie, or run a race, or something until I can understand or cope with what's going on inside me . . . but before she could say a word, a small figure shouldered her way between them.

"Hi, Whitney," Meg muttered. Whitney gave

her the slightest smile and did a quick double take at her dress. But Whitney didn't linger on Meg's appearance. She clearly had other things in mind.

"Would you like to dance, Nick?" Whitney asked in her smokiest tone. Her hair was tightly coiled on the top of her head, which made her eyes look wide and exotic. Her skin was so creamy and her mouth so red that Meg didn't see how any boy could turn her down.

Nick didn't. With one confused look back to Meg, he took Whitney's hand and followed her onto the dance floor.

Meg couldn't watch. The music was so slow and sad, the singer's voice so full of longing, that she had to get out. She knew that if she just looked at Nick with his arms around Whitney, her head resting on his shoulder, her arms around his neck. . . . Something bitter was boiling up inside Meg, and it was a feeling she hated. She suddenly hated Whitney and she hated Nick and she hated herself for feeling this way. When she caught sight of Sean, who was still sitting by himself near the door, she put her head down and pushed her way through the crowd to get to him.

Kids were saying hello to her as she passed. Some commented on how different she looked, and one boy even asked her to dance, but Meg barely heard. Her feet were killing her and her head was screaming and the clicking of Allie's bracelets was driving her crazy. She'd almost reached Sean when she bent down and pulled off Allie's mother's high heels and Allie's plastic bracelets. She was wedging her way through a tight pack of kids when someone stomped sharply on her bare foot.

"OOH!" she cried, the pain surging through her. She hadn't realized how close she was to tears, but there they were, slipping down her cheeks before she knew it.

"I'm sorry," soothed a deep voice.

Meg looked up ever so briefly, but when she saw who it was she felt even more humiliated. It was Mark Coffield, his dark eyes full of regret. Even the scar over his eyebrow seemed to express concern. He wore a pale blue shirt and slim tie that almost made him look like a student teacher. Meg tried to ignore him and get away, but he gently stopped her.

"Are you okay? I really stomped on you," Mark said. He noticed that her shoes were in her hands and frowned even more. "Yow."

"I'm fine," Meg insisted. Mark Coffield was one of the last people she wanted to face right then. She had to get out of there before he saw that she was crying.

But he tipped her chin up with a light touch of his hand and noticed her tears. "Oh, man." He took a perfectly white handkerchief out of his slacks pocket and held it out. Before she could look away he recognized her face. "Hey, it's you! The great runner." He smiled. "I hope I haven't ruined your chances for the Olympics."

Meg's tears were still coming, her foot still stung, and her insides felt raw. She just prayed that Mark wouldn't make any more comments about Nick. She wished he'd never talked to her that day after the run. Maybe if he hadn't noticed her and Nick together, she might never have known how she really felt. Then maybe all five of them would still be together. She stared at Mark's handkerchief. When she didn't take it, he leaned forward and gently dabbed her eyes. His handkerchief came away splotched with brown mascara. Meg started to go.

Mark held on to her arm for one more second. "I'm really sorry. I didn't mean to step on you."

Meg took a deep, shaky breath and shuddered. "Don't worry. Thanks."

Mark put the handkerchief back in his pocket and let go of her arm. Finally she met his eyes. He was staring at her with deep concern. "Are you sure you're okay?"

Meg gave a brief nod. At last she spotted Sean again. He was waiting for her in the doorway. With a wave to Sean, she brushed past Mark and headed for the door.

CHAPTER 14

Celia stared into the mirror in the girls' bathroom and brushed her hair away from her face. Her cheeks were ruddy from two solid sets of dancing and there was a spray of sweat on her upper lip, but she was anxious to get back out on the dance floor again. As long as she kept moving, she could keep all those painful thoughts away and continue to impress everyone with what a great time she was having.

Two other freshmen stood at the mirror next to her. They were both ordinary-looking and trying desperately to help things along with dips and dabs of makeup.

"Diana, he's not going to ask me to dance. I can just tell."

"Give him time, Amy. The dance is only half over."

Celia patted the back of her neck with a wet paper towel and looked at Amy. I envy you,

Amy's expression said in return. Why can't I be dancing every dance like you are? Celia tried to look upbeat — after all, this was everything she'd wanted. She was being noticed and envied. She was one of the popular, chic, pretty girls who guys had to wait to dance with. But then why did she feel so gloomy? Celia gave Amy a sad smile, headed for the stall, and locked the door.

A moment later she heard the freshmen leave and another group of girls enter.

"I need a cigarette," stressed a brassy voice as the bathroom door swung open and closed.

Celia immediately recognized her fellow cheerleader Ann and was about to yell a hello over the stall door when she heard a match being lit and smelled a waft of smoke. Not wanting to be caught with Ann if a teacher came in, Celia didn't make herself known.

"Smoking is gross, Ann," whined a high voice that Celia knew had to be Rebecca.

"Don't hassle me, Becky. I'm not having a good night," Ann grumped back.

"Ann! Just because you're mad about Terry Warner, don't take it out on me."

Now Celia knew she was wise to hide out in the stall. After all the attention Terry'd been paying her, the last thing she needed to do was rub it in by letting Ann know she was eavesdropping. There was a pause in the conversation that was filled in by the shushing of faucets, snapping of makeup cases, brushing, and spritzing.

"Terry Warner," Ann spat out angrily. "He

liked me . . . until Celia started throwing herself at him."

Celia went taut.

"She wasn't throwing herself at him," Rebecca said uncertainly.

"Becky, did you notice the way she was dancing?"

"I don't think so."

Another voice broke in. "Well, you're the only one who didn't, that's for sure."

Celia turned her back to the stall door and put her hands to her face. There was no mistaking the low, husky voice that had just joined Becky's and Ann's. Whitney. But Celia couldn't believe that Whitney would really bad-mouth *her*. It wasn't possible.

There was the sound of spraying and the strong smell of perfume. Whitney's voice continued. "You have to expect some of that when you come from a background like Celia's. You guys should see her house. It makes our garage look like Southfork."

The girls giggled.

"I heard she buys her clothes at those gross secondhand stores," Ann said, sounding less grumpy. "I always said she looked a little used."

"Well, her mom is a hairdresser." Whitney laughed. "I saw her one day at her shop downtown, and she had a blue streak in her hair!"

"No!"

"She looked like a reject from the Muppets."

"She really had a blue streak in her hair?" asked an astonished Rebecca.

"Maybe it was mold."

Rebecca and Ann howled at Whitney's joke.

"I'm telling you guys," Whitney swore, "I only got to be friends with her to get to know Nick. If it wasn't for him, I would have kept my distance."

"Well, thanks a lot, Whitney." Ann's brassiness had returned. "Just because you have the hots for Nick, we're stuck with his cheap cousin for the entire football season." There was a puffy exhalation of smoke and a cough from Rebecca. "Who has some eye shadow I can use real quick? Then we'd better get out of here before Wong catches me."

"Here."

Finally purses were being closed, pantyhose pulled up, faucets turned off, and paper towels pulled.

"Ann," Celia heard Whitney say as the outer door was opened, "you know you should always wear that color shadow. You have such fabulous eyes."

"Really? Sometimes I think they're too close together."

"Oh, no. They're perfect."

The door closed and it was quiet.

Celia wrapped her arms around herself and tried desperately not to make a sound. Her entire body had just broken out in a fine sweat and the perfume and smoke were choking her. She felt she was falling down, down, down, like Alice down the rabbit hole. She was in some dark, frightening place, and there was nothing to hold on to and no way to stop.

"I want my old friends," she whispered.

She knew she sounded like an abandoned child yearning for her mother. That was just how lonely she felt, how lost. Celia was totally alone. She had betrayed her best friend, only to kiss up to a girl who thought nothing of turning around and backstabbing her. How fair. How horrible.

Celia held her tears back by sheer will. If she was leaving this dance now, which she knew she was, there was no way she was walking through that cafeteria with mascara streaming down her face. No. She would hold her head high. She would even smile and say she was tired, that she was going to leave the boys wanting more . . . anything as long as she could get away from Whitney and Ann and Rebecca without any of them ever knowing what she had just overheard.

She pushed open the stall door and caught her reflection in the mirror. Her high color was gone and a few sweaty curls were plastered to her hairline, but other than that she could pass for normal. Someone who really knew her like Meg or Allie would see instantly that she was lost inside, but Whitney and the others would be too busy making cruel jokes to notice.

After splashing a few handfuls of water on her face, Celia pushed open the lavatory door just as a group of seniors were coming in. She squeezed past them, the noise and the crowd hitting her like a harsh wind. As she pushed her way through, she found herself examining every face, searching, praying, hoping. But she didn't see Allie. And even if she did see Allie, what would she say? Now *I* know what it feels like to be backstabbed, too? Celia clenched her fists and forced back her tears as she realized that it was probably hopeless. There was a good chance that Allie would never, ever forgive her.

As Celia slipped quietly out of the cafeteria, she only missed seeing Allie by a dark classroom, an empty walkway, and a few new rose bushes. Allie was close by, sitting with L.P. outside the art bungalows. But even if Celia'd walked right by, Allie might not have noticed her. Because for the first time in weeks, Celia was the furthest thing from Allie's mind.

"It's a mountain of yo-yos," Allie guessed happily.

"Nope."

"Um . . . Oh, I know! It's a squirrel's staircase."

L.P. shook his head again.

"It's all the leftover hamburgers from the cafeteria!"

"Yes!!!!"

Allie laughed, a free bubbly giggle, and of course L.P. laughed, too. They sat on a wooden bench staring at a modern sculpture that had been donated to Redwood High only the week before. It looked amazingly like a messy stack of hockey pucks.

"This is truly inspiring. I'm so glad we came here before the dance," Allie teased.

L.P. grinned. "I thought you'd appreciate it. I figured anybody who could look at that old moose and see a haunted house could tell me what this sculpture is supposed to be."

Allie leaned forward, bathing in the moonlight, the mild wind, and the warmth of L.P.'s smile.

"Maybe you should take a picture of it and have a contest — 'Name This Sculpture.' "

L.P. sprang up, his lanky limbs full of energy. "Actually, I think it has a name already." He crouched down next to it. "Oh, no," he sighed, reading a small metal plate. "You are not going to believe what this is called."

"What?"

L.P. flicked his head, beckoning her over. He was grinning with his hands stuffed in the pockets of the old suit coat he wore over his jeans.

Allie slowly got down on her knees and touched the rough nameplate. "Oh, no. I don't believe it. It's called 'The Pyramid of Learning'?"

" '*The Pyramid of Learning*'!!" they both chanted together. Then at the same time, they sat back on the cool lawn, looked at the sculpture, and laughed.

Allie ran her palms along the blades of grass and leaned back her head. The leaves overhead rustled, and she could hear the band blasting away in the cafeteria. For the first time in weeks, she didn't worry about being too loud, or who would hear her, or if they would think she was silly. Tonight those things didn't seem so important. This whole evening had been so goofy that from the moment L.P. had picked her up, Allie had forgotten to be nervous.

First L.P. had been unable to start his car. They stood there for almost forty minutes, way after Meg and Sean had left, staring into the engine. Finally L.P. had admitted that he didn't know a spark plug from a dipstick but did remember that . . . luckily . . . his older brother

Jed was in the neighborhood visiting a friend. So they'd walked a few blocks and there was Jed, sitting alone on someone's lawn, and the two brothers acted so funny together that Allie wasn't sure what was going on. Then, when they came back to the car, and Jed started it instantly with one flick of his wrist, Allie found herself laughing and laughing — and they started laughing, too, and pretty soon they were all goofy, singing camp songs on the way to school, and making up silly lyrics. When they'd arrived at school, Jed made jokes about being a chauffeur and insisted on taking the car and picking them up later, and the whole thing was so crazy and upside down that it had taken all of Allie's self-consciousness away.

Looking into L.P.'s delighted face, Allie felt an ease she hadn't felt for weeks. She suddenly felt like the old Allie. For the first time since school started, she felt like it was all right to be herself.

"Are you sure you don't mind being so late?" L.P. asked. "I'm sorry that whole thing with the car took so long."

"It was kind of fun." Allie sat very still for a second. The band had just ended one song and was launching into another. "Sounds to me like the dance is still going strong."

L.P. looked down shyly. "Allie. . . ."

He suddenly looked at her with such sweetness and warmth that she had to look away. "What?" she whispered.

He hesitated. "About the whole mess with the car tonight."

"Yes?" Allie smiled. To her it hadn't been a mess, merely an adventure.

"Well, I have kind of a secret to tell you. . . ."

Allie's self-consciousness came rushing back. Secrets just reminded her of Celia and Whitney and that terrible, terrible dark hurt she'd finally been able to get off her mind.

"Secrets are dumb," Allie asserted coldly, starting to walk toward the cafeteria.

L.P. raced to catch up with her. When he did, he made her face him and tentatively took her hand. His palm was dry and warm. "What's the matter?" he asked.

There was a generosity in his eyes that made her realize how she had overreacted. She suddenly sensed that L.P. was a person she could trust. He hadn't minded her laughing when Jed finally started the car. He hadn't lost his temper or ruined their evening, even after the whole frustrating, silly situation. There was something in him she could trust the way she trusted Meg and Nick and Sean. The way she used to trust Celia.

"It's okay," she said very softly. "I just had a friend tell a secret of mine. . . ." She looked into his eyes again, amazed that she was sharing this with him. He was listening as if it were the most important information in the world. "It made me feel really bad. So, I'm kind of sensitive about secrets."

"Well, I don't *have* to tell you," he came back, almost relieved. "As long as you're sure you didn't mind about the car."

"I really didn't. It was just so amazing that your brother was so close by to help."

"Yeah." L.P. shifted. "Amazing." He looked over at the cafeteria and straightened his T-shirt, which had a picture of a huge trout on the front. "Anyway, I'm glad it's all working out."

"Me, too."

"I guess we'd better get over to the dance." He started toward the cafeteria, but stopped when he reached the end of the art building. "So, are you having a good time? Even though it took us an hour to get here?"

Allie felt odd all of a sudden. L.P. was facing her and he still held her hand. She felt so light she might have been made of feathers. "Uh-huh. Are you?"

He smiled and took her other hand. Something about his face almost looked a little scared now, and Allie wrinkled her nose, as if to ask him what he was thinking. But before she could speak, he took a small step toward her and everything inside her head went static. She didn't move as he leaned closer and closer.

Their noses bumped and then their foreheads. But their lips met, slowly, tenderly, for a light, sweet kiss. Allie let her eyes close and was overcome by the softness, the warmth, and the pounding of her own heart.

In that moment, Allie decided it was her best kiss ever.

It was also her first.

CHAPTER
15

Celia flicked on the living room light and threw her jacket on the couch. The house was so quiet that she could hear the kitchen clock ticking and the gas heater coming to life in the corner. Other than that, zero. Obviously her mom wasn't home. Celia felt so alone she would have welcomed her mother's company right now. Even facing the third degree about this disastrous dance would be better than being by herself.

She knelt on the sofa and peeked through the curtains, hoping to see Sean or Meg. But she only spied drawn shades and street lamps — otherwise it was still.

Celia bit her lip. Of course there wasn't anybody there. What did she expect? Besides, what good would Meg or Sean do? Meg'd told her that Whitney was a phony and that spilling Allie's secret was unforgivable. But Celia'd argued and reasoned, refusing to listen or consider that Meg might have been telling the truth. And Sean? What good would he do? Much as he'd want to help, what advice could he possibly give? No, there was little doubt about it. The person Celia really needed to talk to was Allie.

"Stupid," Celia murmured, then she slumped back down into the sofa and wrapped her arms around herself.

She'd give anything if the awful thing she'd done would just vanish so that she and Allie could be friends again. Not friends like Whitney and Rebecca and Ann. Real friends.

"But how can we be friends again if she won't even talk to me!" Celia hollered out loud.

The worst part was that now Celia understood how Allie could cut her off so totally. She understood why Allie wouldn't answer her notes or phone calls or her hellos in the hall. The hurt was too deep. What if Whitney turned around now and told Celia she was sorry and that what happened in the girls' bathroom was all a big joke? Celia would glare in Whitney's face and stomp off.

"If I try one more time, I can at least leave a message. Maybe then she'll listen," Celia prayed out loud.

She'd phoned Allie three times right after that dinner at Nick's, but after Allie'd hung up on her, she hadn't had the nerve to try again. Maybe tonight Allie would hear the sadness in Celia's voice and know that Celia was really, truly sorry.

Celia dialed Allie's number.

Allie's father picked up on the second ring. "Hello?"

Celia was nervous. Her voice felt slightly stuck

and she was wrapping the phone cord frantically around her finger. "Mr. Simon? Hi, it's Celia. Can I talk to Allie?"

She was answered by an odd silence. For a moment Celia wondered if Allie'd told her father what Celia had done to her. She didn't know if she could take Mr. Simon — who'd driven her to swimming lessons when she was nine — yelling at her, too. But when he finally spoke, he didn't sound angry, only surprised, and a little puzzled. "Allie's not here. I thought she was at the dance."

"Is she?" Celia wondered if Allie'd arrived after she left. She could go back to the dance and find her, but that would mean seeing Whitney again. Not knowing what to do, Celia blurted, "I didn't see her there, but I could have missed her. Will you give her a message when she gets — "

Mr. Simon interrupted before she could finish. "What do you mean you didn't see her there?"

"At the dance," Celia clarified. "I didn't see her at the dance."

Another silence.

"I thought Allie went to the dance with you and Meg," Mr. Simon said slowly.

"With me?"

"Celia, are you telling me Allie didn't go to the dance with you?"

The tone in Mr. Simon's voice was sobering. Celia had heard that tone over the summer after she and Allie'd snuck out and taken the bus to the teen fair in San Francisco. She knew instantly that Allie was in hot water, but she had no idea why.

165

"Well, she was probably with Meg," Celia stalled.

"Did you see Meg?"

"Yes. Just for a second, though."

"And was she with Allie?"

"Um, no."

There was a terrible silence. Celia wished she'd never picked up the phone.

"Celia, where's Allie?"

Celia didn't know what to say. Her head was starting to ache, and she had no idea what answer would help Allie most. "I don't know. She didn't go to the dance with me," she admitted, too confused to lie. "We kind of had a fight a couple weeks ago. . . ."

"All right, Celia, Allie will talk to you later."

"But I'm sure there's no problem. I'm sure she's okay."

"Fine."

"Tell her I called."

There was a click and the line went dead.

It was a slow dance. The last of the third set. After this, the band would take their final break, come back and play five or six more songs, and then it would be over. As Allie swayed to the music, her forehead resting on L.P.'s shoulder, she didn't know how she could bear for this night to end.

"Hey, I haven't stepped on your feet once, have I?" L.P. asked, amazed.

Allie looked up into his face. He was smiling down at her, his eyes looking more delighted from the reflection of the colored lights. "I don't think so."

Then she grinned and put her feet on top of his, like she used to do with her father when she was little. L.P. wore leather court shoes, and she was in soft turquoise flats, but he made a mock face as if her weight were killing him. Still they danced like that, taking funny stiff steps over the paper leaves and the occasional fallen streamer, until they both laughed.

After that she laid her cheek against his smooth lapel and hummed along with the song. It was okay to hum with L.P. or even sing. She'd learned that right away in the car with his brother. The goofier she got, the more L.P. seemed to enjoy himself.

"So where are your friends?" L.P. whispered.

On the way over to the cafeteria, Allie'd told L.P. about Meg and Sean and Nick. She'd also told him more about Celia and how much it hurt that their friendship had ended. Of course, she'd left out the details of her secret, and L.P. had never brought up his secret again, but none of that seemed very important now.

Allie lifted her head and looked around. "I don't know where Meg and Sean went. I guess maybe they left before we got here."

"I think I met Meg once when I went by the Haunted House. She was really nice."

Allie nodded. "There's Nick."

They both craned their necks to see him. Nick didn't look like he was having a good time. He was dancing with Whitney, one arm hanging limply around her waist. But as much as Whitney seemed to be trying to gaze into his eyes, he almost never looked at her. When he saw Allie, he waved and smiled — the first smile Allie'd seen on him. Whitney looked over, too, but before Whitney could glare at her, Allie hid her face by resting her cheek against L.P. Even Whitney Hain couldn't spoil the ease and warmth and softness Allie felt inside.

Allie did notice when Ann, the sophomore cheerleader, pushed her way through the dancers, tapped Whitney's shoulder, and whispered something in Whitney's ear. Allie saw Whitney giggle and Nick walk away looking relieved that he could leave the dance floor and join his male buddies. And Allie was aware that Ann and Whitney were practically running back over to the front door. But she didn't give it her total attention. There was too much competition from the slow, sweet music and the fresh, piny smell of L.P.'s skin. But when Allie saw Whitney and Ann emerge from the crowd again and march across the dance floor in her direction, everything came back into startlingly clear focus.

Allie pulled back from L.P. and stopped dancing. He looked puzzled, but finally noticed the cheerleaders.

"Hi, Allie," Whitney said first. She was projecting over the music and everything about her posture and voice was hard. The two couples next to them danced farther away as if they sensed the danger. Allie didn't reply. She merely stared. She'd always thought Whitney was beautiful, but now that tiny mouth reminded Allie of a sour cherry.

Ann stepped up next to Whitney. "Having a good time?" she asked in a sing-song voice.

"Yes," Allie answered proudly. She turned away from them, took L.P.'s hand, and started dancing again. He was holding her firmly and attempted to steer her away, but Ann slipped around to their other side and stopped him.

"We have a message for you," Ann grinned.

Allie let go of L.P. and stopped. WHAT? she almost yelled. That I wore a bra under my bathing suit? Big deal! Go ahead, tell L.P. that I'm a baby, a loser, a fool. He knows that you two are the real fools, and that I'm okay. At least, I think he does. So go ahead, tell my dumb secret, and then leave me alone!

Whitney stepped forward. "We just wanted to tell you that there's someone looking for you."

The coolness in Whitney's voice made Allie's insides change from anger to fear. Was she being set up? Was Celia lurking somewhere, hiding out so she could surprise Allie and do something even more underhanded and cruel? Allie could barely stand that thought. Even though Celia had betrayed her so terribly, Allie secretly believed that there had to be a good reason — an excuse — that deep down Celia would never have wanted to hurt her like that.

The music ended and the dancers wandered slowly off the floor. As they did, Allie saw a balding man in a white shirt and a golf jacket sidling his way between two couples. Allie stared at him for a moment. It didn't make sense — seeing him against the streamers and the paper grapes and the colored lights. It was so out of context . . . so wrong . . . so totally mixed up.

He walked right up to her. "Allie," he said angrily.

"Dad!"

For a second Allie couldn't put it together. Her father at the dance — in front of Whitney and Ann and L.P. — it was too horrible to be real.

"I want to talk to you," her father insisted. His face reddened as he looked around at the other kids. "I'll wait outside. I expect you out there in two minutes."

He gave her a severe look, and with a quick turn marched back toward the door.

"I want to talk to you," imitated Ann in a sappy voice.

"Aww, he's worried about his baby," added Whitney.

L.P., who was looking back and forth between Allie and the cafeteria door, took a step toward Whitney and Ann. "Why don't you two get lost," he muttered.

They both giggled and gave him coy smiles but ran back to Rebecca. As they did, Allie could see other girls joining them and beginning to point and laugh. They reminded her of a swarm of bees, buzzing and circling and stinging as viciously as they could.

L.P. turned back to Allie and put his hand on her shoulders. He looked puzzled and a little worried. "What's your dad doing here?"

Allie suddenly couldn't deal with one more thing that hurt this way. She knew she could start sobbing any minute, and she just wanted to get away from it all before it got any worse. Not looking right or left, she marched toward the exit.

L.P. stuck by her. "Allie. Tell me what's going on? Is it my fault?"

She stopped just before the doorway and looked at him. He was running his hand through his short hair, making it stand up in about eight different directions.

"Of course it's not your fault," she managed, clenching back the tears. "But it's better if I just go on home. Really."

They made it outside, and Allie was momentarily comforted by the cool darkness. Then she saw her father waiting by the outdoor window to the student store, and she walked over to him. The tears were running down her face, although she didn't heave or sob. She felt too empty for that, too defeated. All she wanted now was to go home and be left in peace.

L.P. trailed anxiously. Mr. Simon started to grab Allie's elbow to go, but L.P. couldn't stand it. He wasn't sure what this whole thing was about, but he couldn't stand seeing Allie cry, and he didn't want her to face it alone.

"Mr. Simon," he insisted. Allie's father turned around. He was short and stocky, with a round face. If he weren't so angry, he might have reminded L.P. of cheery Mr. Greengrocer, who announced the sales on TV for Albertson's market. "Hello, sir, I'm L.P. Brubaker," he continued, putting his hand out to shake. He wasn't quite sure if it was the right thing to do, but he was trying to figure the whole thing out. For the first time he found himself regretting his slightly punk haircut and silly trout T-shirt.

"I'm sorry to break up your date," Allie's father stated curtly. "But she has rules about who she rides in a car with, and she knows that."

Uh-oh, L.P. thought. His hand dropped back down to his side, and there was a hardness in his stomach the size of a softball. He was beginning to wonder if what was going on really was his fault. Had Allie's father somehow found out that he was only fifteen and a half and had driven alone with a learner's permit? But who could have told him? Whitney? His brother? L.P. couldn't figure it out. All he knew was that if he did find out he was going to kill . . . if he didn't die of shame first. Which was the more likely thing to happen now that he thought about Mr. Simon revealing the truth about his dumb stunt to Allie.

L.P. shuddered. He didn't understand all that much about girls, but he did know that what had just gone on in the gym with Whitney was one of those awful things that rich, snobby girls do to girls who are different like Allie. And Allie had just told him how she'd been hurt once already, and here he was practically pointing her out to be humiliated again. L.P. was suddenly so ashamed of himself that he couldn't look Allie in the face.

"Good-night," Mr. Simon said as he started to lead Allie away.

L.P. thought about running after her and apologizing. But what could he say? Soon enough she would know the truth and realize that he was the one to blame. It was all his fault that she had been pointed out and made fun of. Just the thought of it made him want to hide his face and disappear.

Allie and her father were trudging off toward the parking lot. No good-night. Not even a regretful look back. Just the shuffling of feet against concrete and the dark emptiness of the fall sky. L.P. stood there feeling worse and worse, smaller, and more guilty.

Knowing that he had just lost something very special, he kicked his heel in the cold dirt and watched Allie go.

CHAPTER 16

Over the next few weeks the last traces of summer left. The leaves fell off the old oak that held up the tree house. They made big piles that none of the friends cleaned up.

Meg spent almost all her free time now on the freshman fundraiser. Inside the Haunted House, the frantic activity kept things warm. Hammers tapped. Brooms whisked. Footsteps clattered up and down the stairs, voices boomed from room to room, and the air smelled of fresh pumpkins and paint.

After so many weeks of scrubbing and scraping, borrowing and begging, getting covered with spackle and glue, enduring smashed fingers and orange-dabbed hair, the Haunted House was actually coming together. Now, with only four more after-school work sessions left, Meg could only hope.

She stood just inside the living room and

marveled at the transformation. Drapes were in position over the doorways, and papier-mâché witches' heads decorated the wall. One corner of the living room was filled with pumpkins, while in the other there were racks of costumes and masks made by the art classes.

The only thing that was the same as before was the old moose head above the fireplace . . . and even that seemed as if it had changed. After weeks of watching all the commotion — the building up and the tearing down that had gone on under his big nose — the moose looked proud, but sad. Meg had decided she was starting to feel an awful lot like that old moose.

The moose had watched as his familiar surroundings were torn apart and rearranged; Meg felt she had seen the same thing happen with her friends. Since the dance, she'd begun to realize that she couldn't force Nick to feel differently about her by wearing some eye shadow and a borrowed dress, any more than she could force her friends to stay together. It had taken a while for her to understand. But after nights of crying alone in her room, she had cried herself out. She was beginning to think that she just had to accept the changes they were all going through and let the rest go.

So Meg had almost given up on getting Allie and Celia back together. That seemed almost impossible. Plus there was another big problem for Allie . . . L.P. Since the dance, Allie had been too ashamed to talk to him, and from what Meg could see, L.P. was just as embarrassed. Over the last few weeks, Allie and L.P. had barely

175

exchanged hellos; so now there were two people that Allie couldn't talk to — her former best friend, and the boy she was probably crazy about.

Celia, of course, was having a hard time, too. Except for the football games, she was avoiding Whitney and the other cheerleaders. It was another crazy situation like Allie's. Celia told Meg that she was too ashamed to admit that she had overheard the girls talking in the bathroom, but not brave enough to tell them off. Meanwhile, Celia was at least trying to talk to Allie, but it was almost hopeless. Whenever Celia called out to her in the halls, Allie pretended she didn't hear her and stomped off. Meg was beginning to think more and more that Allie was being unreasonable. As much as Meg didn't like the way Celia had acted, she had learned her lesson by now.

The one good thing for all of them in the last few weeks had been the Haunted House. At least when her friends came up to her with looks on their faces that said they wished they could go back to middle school, Meg could stick a torn costume or a paintbrush in their hands and tell them to work. Allie came in almost every day at lunch, and Sean and Celia helped after school. Nick was the only one who hadn't contributed much.

In a way, Meg was glad. Since the football team was playing so poorly, he had tons of extra practice. In gym the girls and boys were still split up, and most lunch periods she worked on the Haunted House, so she only had to see Nick in class or sometimes in the halls. She still thought about him all the time, but not seeing as much of him made things easier. When they did run into each other, they'd chat about homework or midterms, the Haunted House or football. The old intensity and intimacy was gone, but as much as Meg missed it, it also made things a lot less painful.

"Meg, are we still going to do the living head on the platter?"

John Purdy's voice cut into Meg's thoughts, and she turned to look at him. How she had managed to daydream for so long in the middle of all this commotion was a mystery.

"Sure, John. Check with Marcie Hamilton and Mr. Kentfield upstairs. They have the details."

As John walked off, Meg spotted Hilda Levi, a tiny freshman from her English class, who was trying to haul an aluminum ladder across the living room. It was obvious that the back end of the ladder didn't know what the front end was doing. When Hilda turned around, five other freshmen and two teachers had to duck.

"Hilda, watch out!"

Sean, who was trying on a rented skeleton suit, stuck a skinny arm up just in time to prevent one end of the ladder from going through the front window. With the help of Mr. Barnes, the bulky gymnastics coach, the two of them took the ladder from Hilda and leaned it against the wall.

"Whew," Meg breathed. She started stenciling letters on a piece of poster board and wondered if this all was actually going to get done.

"Meg, when do you want the janitors to bring over the tables?" asked Sam Pond, who was practicing scary faces in front of a pocket mirror.

That was another thing to think about. The tables had to be set up outside for the refreshments, and Meg tried to remember if she'd asked Helen Pyne's father, who owned the local Safeway, if he would donate the apples.

"I don't know yet, Sam, I'll let you know."

Sam signaled okay and then disappeared around the corner. Meg was back at work for only a moment when she was distracted again.

"Meg, Miss Meyer's taking me downtown to get some doughnuts. What kind do you want?"

Meg looked up to the top of the stairs. It was Celia. The newest, but most hardworking, helper. There she stood with her blonde hair in a scarf, wearing an apron that was stiff with glue, tugging off a pair of rubber gloves.

Meg halted her sign lettering and flicked her braids behind her shoulders. "A glazed one and some milk for me."

"I want one of those orange and green cupcakes," Sean said.

"Gross," Celia and Meg commented at the same time.

Sean laughed. "Where's your Halloween spirit?"

Celia clomped the rest of the way down the stairs and flopped her gloves down on the old chair that sat in the corner.

Meg looked at her friend thoughtfully. "Celia, are you sure that you're going to be able to do the tickets on Halloween night?"

Celia nodded. "Absolutely." She stretched and brushed back a strand of hair. "Anybody else want anything from Winchell's? I'm going!" she yelled to all parts of the house. Not getting an answer, she turned her back to the screen door and knocked it open.

But as she did, someone grabbed the door from the outside and held it. It was Allie. For a moment the two girls stood in the doorway paralyzed. They stared at each other as if they both were ghosts, then acted super polite.

"Hi," Celia said hopefully.

But Allie brushed past her and ran up to Meg. As she did, Sean pulled off his skeleton mask and joined them.

"You better not let your father see you around here," he cautioned.

Allie shook her head and her unicorn barrettes wobbled. "I'm out of jail," she said, raising her arms, but still excluding Celia. "I'm not grounded anymore!"

Celia was standing uncomfortably in the doorway. "That's great, Al."

Allie looked at Celia with a cold expression, then turned back to face Meg and Sean.

Her eyes watering at Allie's coolness, Celia started to go.

"Wait, Celia," Meg urged, "don't go — "

"Miss Meyer is waiting," Celia countered before Meg could finish. With that, the screen door banged shut.

"Boy, people are sure coming and going a lot around this place," Sean tried to joke.

Now it was Allie who looked forlorn. She stared after the screen door and twisted her pink beads. "I guess I'd better not stick around." Allie moped.

"Why?"

"I'll come back at lunch tomorrow. When she's not here."

Meg and Sean exchanged looks.

"I just wanted to let you know I wasn't grounded anymore."

Meg walked up to Allie. "Wait. That means you can work Halloween night. Right?"

Allie nodded.

Sean joined them. He had his mask under his arm and his freckled face looked mischievous. "Hey, Meg," he hinted, "I know just what job we need Allie to do."

"What's that?"

Sean bumped her with his elbow. "Take tickets."

Sean was looking at her as if she were supposed to get some secret meaning, and for a second Meg just stared at him. Then it hit her. Of course. Celia was taking tickets. If Allie was the other ticket-taker, at least they'd be forced to sit together. Meg almost laughed as she realized that now that she'd almost given up trying to hold things together, here was Sean stepping in and taking her place.

"So, Al," Meg agreed, "can I sign you up?"

"Yeah," Sean conspired, "will you take tickets?"

Allie was still staring spacily out the screen door. "Oh, sure," she answered finally. "I'll do whatever you want me to." She slipped on her jeans jacket. "I guess I'd better go home. I told my mom I'd only be gone for an hour. I promised her I wouldn't make my dad freak out again. I'll get all the details from you tomorrow at lunch."

"Great," Meg cried. She and Sean opened the front door and escorted Allie out.

After Allie'd walked over the tall grass and into the quad, Meg put her arm around Sean. "You know, Pendleton, you're pretty devious."

"I am?"

"Yeah. But you're also pretty smart."

"Think so?" Sean said a little smugly, and then the two friends giggled, doing their best imitation of a fiendish laugh.

An hour and a half later, Sean was trudging his way across the grassy field and away from the Haunted House. He had deliberately avoided walking home with Meg because he had a good idea. It was such a good idea that Sean was actually singing the new Springsteen song under his breath as he walked along.

If he could bring Celia and Allie together at the Haunted House, then Sean wanted to make doubly sure that they were *all* there. He was certain that if he could just ask Nick, he would be willing to come, too. But the way things were going he couldn't bet on seeing him in the hallways before Friday. No, the only thing to do was go find Nick himself . . . right now, while he knew where he was. That didn't take much guessing. Even from the Haunted House you could hear the smack and the thump of shoulder pads.

Sean was there in another five minutes. Standing on the sideline along with the coaches and the other squads of players, he watched as the players lined up and ran their plays.

"Hit him, Baldwin, hit him," the coach yelled.

Sean could barely see between the players, so he couldn't tell who the coach wanted hit. It was like standing in the middle of a forest. Sean picked his way around the players, trying to find a better view.

"Hey, look at Warner. He's got the ball."

Sean looked out again and saw that some poor guy was lying on the field under a pile of about ten guys. He looked more like he'd swallowed the football than anything else. Sean shook his head.

"Wow."

"What's that?"

"Ugh," Sean went on without thinking, "I was just saying I'm glad I'm not under that pile."

The player next to him grunted under his helmet and then started watching the action again.

"Think you guys will ever win?" Sean asked casually.

The player didn't look at him but slowly removed his helmet. It was Jay Creary. There was black painted under his eyes and his hair was plastered over his forehead. Sean decided not to let Jay get to him. He fantasized how in ten years he'd be inventing some great new video game, while Jay would be pumping gas at the downtown Mobil station. That thought brought a smile to Sean's face.

"What's so funny?" Jay growled immediately. He narrowed his eyes in a wordless threat, and Sean took a step back.

"Nothing. I came to talk to Nick. Could you tell him I'm here?"

But before he could step back again, Jay grabbed the front of Sean's jacket and was twisting it with his fist. It didn't really hurt, but Sean worried that his jacket would rip and he would have to explain what happened to his parents. In that instant Sean spotted Nick standing down the line. "Nick," he choked. "Nick!" But Nick looked right past him and ran back out onto the field. At the same time, Jay let him go.

Sean straightened his jacket and looked back across the field. He wasn't sure if Nick hadn't seen him or was actually ignoring him. Either way, it made his chest pound and his eyes sting. He'd given up and was starting to walk away when he felt Jay's fat hand on his shoulder.

"Hey, ankle-biter," Jay growled.

"What?"

"Do me a favor. Don't ever let me see your ugly face again."

Sean thought of telling Jay exactly what he thought of him, but he could feel Jay's steamy breath down his collar and the pressure of his hand on his shoulder.

"Got that?" Jay insisted.

"Yeah," Sean grumbled, backing away. He tried once more to look for Nick. But the guys were all in helmets and uniforms and he couldn't tell one from another. Throwing up his hands in disappointment, Sean turned around and walked away.

CHAPTER 17

"Happy Halloween," Meg whispered to herself. "It sure feels scary enough right now."

She leaned on the sink in the upstairs bathroom of the Haunted House. The doors were due to open in fifteen minutes, and she'd been working on the finishing touches all day. This was the first time she'd been alone since early that morning.

A papier-mâché black cat looked down at her from over the mirror and a jack-o'-lantern grinned expectantly from atop a small shelf. She tried to smile back at them, but she couldn't quite get the corners of her mouth to cooperate. She could hear the drama students rehearsing their boos and cackles in the rooms on either side. Miss Meyer was outside yelling to be careful with the candles and there were heavy footsteps from downstairs that could only belong to Franken-stein. Even through the walls, Meg could feel the collective excitement and expectation.

This whole enterprise was scary, Meg realized, and yet exhilarating. It was like the first time she'd climbed to the top of the tree house. She'd worked so hard to build it, but then she was a little afraid to climb all the way to the top — afraid she'd fall, afraid she'd look like a fool when she climbed, afraid she'd get up there and not be able to look down. Now, even though she was proud of herself and all the other freshmen who'd worked on the house, she was scared it would be a flop and that when they opened the doors no one would be waiting to come in.

Meg stared at herself in the mirror. She unbraided her hair and let it fall in even waves down her back. She was in her jeans and pink lacy T-shirt that Celia'd given her for her birthday and a baggy suit jacket of her dad's. Most everybody else was in costume, but Meg hadn't had time to go home and change. Besides, there was something about this funky, thrown-together outfit that suited her — much more than her attempt at the dance to look like a *femme fatale*. There was something inside her that made her want to face this evening as herself.

"Okay. Here we go," she chanted, giving her hair one more pat.

She opened the door and walked slowly down the upstairs hall. She peeked in each room at the scenes that were being set up — the famous head on a platter, Dracula and his victim, witches over a caldron. Everybody was rushing and chattering, checking last minute notes, readjusting noses, and trying to get hats to stay on.

"Good luck," Meg called as she skipped downstairs. She was answered by eerie shrieks and hoots.

Sean was waiting for her. His skeleton suit hung baggily on his skinny frame. He was holding up the pants so as not to trip on the cuffs and had his mask tucked in the crook of his arm.

"Everything's ready in the basement," he reported. His voice was unstable with anticipation and his red hair messy from his mask.

"Is Barnes down there?" Meg asked. Since the goblins in the basement was rather a free-for-all, Meyer and the principal had insisted that a teacher be down there at all times. Meg knew that the gymnastic coach's stocky frame and tough personality would keep everything under control.

"Yeah." Sean nodded. "He's been trying to teach Sam Pond to walk on his hands."

"Great. We open the doors in a few minutes, so turn on the black light, and get everybody ready." Sean saluted happily and rushed downstairs.

Meg surveyed the first floor. There was a fortune-teller — Mrs. Davidson, who taught home ec — and the monster corner, where Frankenstein, Wolfman, and something out of *Star Wars* practiced their deep voices and clumsy gestures. There were also rows of chairs set up for kids to listen to the drama teacher tell scary stories.

Blocking the front door was a long table covered with rolls of tickets, empty coffee cans, and gray metal money boxes. Celia and Allie had arrived, but contrary to Meg's hopes, the two girls were still not speaking. They managed to sit at opposite ends of the table facing different ways,

186

as if catching a glimpse of one another were too painful. In between sat Mrs. Briggs, the elderly teacher in charge of the money.

"Ready?" Meg asked as she walked over and leaned on the table.

Celia and Allie both looked up, as if they were trying to figure out which one of them Meg was addressing. Neither wanted to respond if the other was participating in the conversation. Celia was dressed in a long, old, melon-colored satin gown — a prime thrift store find, Meg guessed, and she was the one to finally answer, "I think so."

As Meg spoke Allie put her head down and counted the quarters in her gray box.

"How about you, Al?"

Allie'd come as a flapper and seemed to be wearing every piece of plastic jewelry she owned. "Sure."

Meg's stomach clenched. After all the meeting and planning, working and hoping, praying and figuring, the moment had come. Trying not to let Allie and Celia see just how terrified she was, she turned her back on them and slowly opened the front door.

As she did her insides felt electric, as if a current were running through her, like those silly models they used in science class. It was a perfect night — dark and breezy with a round, glowing moon. The front of the house was all lit up, and it cast shadows almost to the quad. Rows of tables were set up for pumpkin carving, and there were boxes of cupcakes and huge metal containers of punch. At least thirty freshmen were manning the refreshment tables and the buckets for apple-bobbing, and there was even a section roped off where you could throw water balloons at Mr. Casey, the physics teacher. But Meg's thrill wasn't only because of the efforts of her classmates and friends. She appreciated more than anyone all the organized activity and the neat row of tables and the smell of cloves and vanilla candles. But beyond the tables and freshmen, held back by a rope and two stanchions, there was a sight that was even better.

A line stretched from the porch to the edge of the quad, a line of at least two hundred students. And behind them Meg could see couples and groups wandering over from the parking lot, heading for the line at the back. She spotted some costumes — a clown, a punker, an incredible outfit that looked like a strawberry. Many of the kids weren't in costume, but Meg could tell by the way they craned anxiously to get a look at the house, and the sound of their voices, that they were just as excited.

She put both hands to her mouth to cover her obvious grin, and looked at Miss Meyer, who gave her a proud wink. All Meg could think was after all the crazy, awful, painful things that had happened these first two months at Redwood, finally . . . finally something had gone right!

Allie knew her idea was a terrific success. Meg had told her, and that had meant a lot, but there was other evidence, too. She knew it by the anticipation in their eyes as they came in, the smiles on kids' faces as they walked out. She knew it by the full bubbly pride she felt inside and the way

Miss Meyer kept coming up and patting her shoulder and the nonstop glow in Meg's eyes.

And she knew by the wad of money in her gray metal box — so thick that old Mrs. Briggs had to keep taking bills out to stack and count and stuff into her cloth bank sack. Allie knew that every time she looked at the stadium lights for the next four years she would remember that she'd had a great idea.

"Do you have any quarters?" she heard Celia ask. Allie had two rolls but she didn't respond. The weird thing was the more she tried to block Celia out, the more aware of her she became. It was as if every gesture, every word that Celia uttered, entered Allie's brain through the side of her head.

Not glancing up, Allie took a roll of coins and handed it to Mrs. Briggs. "Give this to Celia," Allie said coolly. Then she tore off a ticket and smiled, ready to sell it to the next person in line.

But when she looked up her heart bounced, even more alarmingly than when she had to deal with Celia. Standing in front of her, wearing a T-shirt with whales on it and a pair of bobbing antennae topped with bright blue nobs, was L.P. He was with two other sophomore boys, one wearing a pair of huge sunglasses. The other was in whiteface and mimed that he was not speaking.

L.P.'s friends bought their tickets and moved in, but even though there was still a line behind him, L.P. lingered. He looked down at Allie and his coiled wire antennae danced. A little embarrassed, he reached up and took his headpiece off.

"Hi, Allie."

Allie had run into L.P. a few times at school but didn't know what to say. Every time she saw him her embarrassment came flooding back, and she knew from the way he reacted that he felt the same way. Thinking about how awful it must have been for him to have her father come into the cafeteria and drag her away made it hard to look L.P. in the face.

"Hi." She tore more tickets off, placing them in neat piles of five.

"The house looks pretty haunted."

Allie thought about telling him to move ahead, that he was keeping other people waiting. But the words wouldn't come out.

L.P. looked up at the wall behind her. "I'm glad the moose is still up. It's the only thing that looks the same as before."

Allie almost smiled. Suddenly the memory of meeting L.P. in here that first day came racing back. She'd been so nervous, on such unfamiliar ground, and he was so wacky and charming. Even though that first meeting had ended so dreadfully, she'd known when she first saw him that he was someone special. Allie tried to wipe those thoughts away, but when she looked up again, L.P. was still standing there. Kids were nudging and muttering from behind, annoyed by the delay.

"Allie, do you think maybe we could talk for a few minutes tonight?"

L.P.'s eyes seemed a little frightened, and he couldn't quite look at her. When she gazed up at him, the rest of the crowd seemed to blur. Only

190

his face was clearly visible. "I have to work until we close."

L.P. shifted and banged his antennae against his other palm. "I could meet you then. When does the house close?"

Suddenly Allie wondered if there was hope. L.P.'s voice was so sweet, and she couldn't help thinking about the dance and the goofy ride with his brother and drinking coffee downtown. But she had to go right home after the Haunted House, and although she was no longer grounded, she was still "on probation," as her father called it. "Ten o'clock. But I have to go right home."

"Oh. I see." L.P. stood there for one more awkward minute until a rowdy voice from the back — Allie suspected it was football player Jay Creary — yelled for whoever was at the front to get his behind moving.

L.P. squinted back, saw Jay, and gave Allie a sad smile. A moment later he was gone.

It was a long evening for Sean. When he'd first thought of staying down in that basement all night in a skeleton suit, jumping out and scaring people, it sounded great — like something David Byrne or Eddie Van Halen would do. What he hadn't considered was the fact that the old heating system was in the basement, and the hood to his costume had almost no ventilation, and that after two and half hours of this he would be dripping with sweat and dying to get it over with.

He could tell that his fellow goblins were just as fed up and glad that in fifteen minutes they'd close up shop and go home. Sam Pond hadn't walked on his hands for the last hour, the Swain twins and Nancy Carlin hadn't bothered scaring the last group to come down, and even Mr. Barnes was looking peaked.

For the last few minutes, there hadn't been one visitor, so Barnes stood up, wiped the heavy sweat from his face, and announced wearily, "Who wants punch?"

Six goblin hands went up.

"Can I help you get it?" Dan Kremer asked hopefully, pulling off his mask. Barnes nodded, and the two went up the stairs.

Sean leaned back against the wall and eased himself down. The front of his mask was damp from his breathing, and he was thinking of calling it a night and sneaking outside himself when he heard voices coming down the stairs and saw another group of kids coming into the goblin room. Deciding to leave the spooking to the Swains or Nancy, he didn't budge until he recognized who it was and slowly stood.

"So what's so scary about this?" Jay Creary complained with a choppy laugh.

He was accompanied by Terry Warner, Gus Baldwin, and Bill Bloodgood, all of them beefy upperclassmen. As soon as they entered the over-heated basement they took off their letterman's jackets.

"Ellen Levine is too perfect as a monster. She should dress like that all the time."

Sean didn't have to squint through his mask to recognize that cutting voice and the accompanying giggles. The voice belonged to Whitney and the giggles were coming from her friends Rebecca and Ann. But what was even more distressing was that Nick was with them. He wore this old Davey Crockett jacket and hat that Sean recognized from their trip to Disneyland two summers before. He was the only one who'd attempted a costume.

"Did you see the number of tickets they've sold?" Nick said excitedly. "I bet those lights are up by our next game."

"Just as long as they don't call 'em freshman lights," complained Jay. He was already sweating and rubbed his upper lip with the sleeve of his jacket. "They could call 'em the ankle-biter lights. Right, Gus?"

Gus and Bill laughed.

Sean couldn't take it anymore. He was hot and tired and near the breaking point, and he knew this might be his only chance to show Nick that he was not somebody to be ignored. He could stand up to guys like this. After the way he'd been treated on the football field a few days ago, he'd had enough of Jay and his bullying. Besides, his class had worked too hard to be put down. He wasn't a wimp or a joke. He was still smarter than all these guys put together, and Nick had to realize that.

Sean whipped off his mask and walked right up to Jay. "What do you care what the lights are called, Creary?" Jay stared at Sean, astonished. Nick stared, too. Sean felt himself smile just a little. For some glorious reason, his voice had stayed perfectly even. "Maybe they'll help you see so you can finally win a game," he added for good measure.

Sean had barely finished his sentence when he

felt himself being lifted by the shoulders of his costume. The underarm seams were digging into his flesh like wires and there was a loud rip of fabric up the back. Then Jay dropped him back down like a discarded trash bag, and Sean saw a fist that looked as big as a cantaloupe no more than five inches from his mouth.

"Cool it, Jay!" Nick yelled, running over.

Jay took a step back, but his face was red and quivering and his fist still hung on to Sean's collar. Nick got between Jay and Sean but didn't seem to know what to do next. "Jay, leave him alone."

Sean looked at Nick, but Nick wouldn't look back. And then it hit Sean . . . *Nick doesn't know what to do. Nick is just as chicken and confused as I am!* That thought scared him as much as Jay did; probably even more. For now he realized that Nick didn't know everything. Nick couldn't do everything. Nick got intimidated just like the rest of them. In fact, maybe Nick didn't like Jay but he was too scared to stand up for the class. Well, somebody had to do it. Somebody had to say, "Enough."

Sean looked away from Nick and back to Jay's big beefy face. He slowly shook his head. "Go ahead, Jay," he taunted. "Slug me if it will make you feel better about yourself. Everybody knows you have an inferiority complex bigger than your fat head."

There were gasps. Nick went pale. Jay raised his fist.

"Why you — "

Just then the door exploded from upstairs and

194

there was a clattering of anxious footsteps. Everyone jumped. Even Jay loosened his fist and anxiously watched the stairs to see if it was Mr. Barnes. They were all relieved to find it was only Meg, followed by Celia and Allie. "What's going on?" Meg asked as soon as she reached the bottom step.

Silence.

"Somebody tell me what's going on," Meg pushed.

"Nothing," Sean grumbled finally.

Jay let out one deep laugh. "Yeah. We just got scared, that's all. Isn't that what's supposed to happen down here?"

"That's not what it sounded like to me."

Whitney, arms folded and looking very assured, approached the girls. "Really, Meg," she said coyly. "Sean just scared himself. You should have known that would happen when you put your reject friend down here. He's really so lame. . . ."

But now Celia was stepping in front of Meg and was practically nose to nose with Whitney. "WHO ARE YOU CALLING A REJECT?" she demanded.

Whitney leaned back against the railing in shock. The goblins, the ball players, and the cheerleaders were all staring openmouthed at the two girls.

"You called my friend a reject," Celia went on, her eyes full of fire. "Well, he's not. I think you owe him an apology."

"An apology! Him apologizing to me and Jay is more like it. I know he's your dear friend,

195

Celia, but even you have to admit he is truly pathetic and has no right to talk to us like that."

Celia looked like she was ready to explode. "I wouldn't talk about pathetic if I were you. Sean is a million times a better person and a better friend than you'll ever be."

"And what's that supposed to mean?"

"He would never use people like you do."

"When did I ever use anybody?"

"You were never my friend, Whitney. You just used me because you have a crush on Nick and you thought I could help you get to know him."

Nick took a step forward with a stunned expression.

Whitney tried to grab the banister and fumbled for a moment. Her pale skin was crimson with rage. "You'd better watch it, Celia," she rasped. "You only made cheerleader because I was your partner. If you think you'll make it again next year, you just wait and see."

"That's right," Ann piped up, stepping across and putting a hand on Whitney's arm.

Celia glared at Rebecca and then at Ann. She shook her head. "Go on. Take her side," she said disgustedly. "You should hear the way she talks about you behind your back."

Celia pushed past her. She took Sean by the arm and began guiding him toward the stairs. Ignoring the looks and the murmurs, she pushed him along. There was only one person in the whole room who could stop her.

"Cici."

Celia froze at the sound of Allie's voice.

"What?" she shot back, half expecting she'd have to defend herself again.

Allie looked her straight in the eye. "I'm coming, too," she said softly.

There was a moment of pure silence. Then Celia managed to smile. "Good," she said. "Let's get out of here."

Taking Sean with them, the two girls headed up the stairs.

CHAPTER 18

Meg stood alone in the farmhouse kitchen and drank three cups of punch, one right after the other. Usually she hated drinking sweet stuff like that, but she'd been working so hard and was so stunned from the scene in the basement that she could have swallowed every sugary leftover sitting on the kitchen counter.

Miraculously, what Meg now realized had almost been a fight had passed undetected. The scene had broken up by the time Barnes returned, and luckily, old Mrs. Briggs was too hard of hearing to notice anything unusual. At least the success of the Haunted House had not been marred. Now Sean was outside taking down tables; Jay, Whitney, and the others had left; and Celia and Allie were sitting quietly together counting the money.

It was over. Disaster had come close, but decided not to pay a visit. It had passed by, all was well, and finally, Meg could go home. Relieved and still hungry, she took a frosted cookie and another cup of punch.

Before she could finish, the door slowly opened and a head of golden hair appeared.

"Oh. Hi, Meg."

It was Nick. His Davey Crockett hat was in his hand, and his jacket was slung over his shoulder. His eyes looked sad. When he came in his posture had none of its usual springiness. He entered slowly, cautiously, as if he were walking barefoot over sharp rocks. "Have you seen Sean?"

Meg put down her cup and stared. Her insides started to go haywire, but she forced herself to look at him. For the first time she saw in Nick an unsureness that matched her own. "He's outside cleaning up."

Nick started for the door.

"Nick, he told me he wanted to be left alone. Don't rub it in."

"What's that supposed to mean?" Nick asked, his voice surprised and defensive.

As soon as Sean told her what had happened in the basement, Meg realized that it was an attempt to impress Nick. Why were they both trying to impress Nick all the time! Neither of them were that important to Nick anymore — Nick had football and Whitney and his bully pals from the team. Maybe it was time for both her and Sean to face the facts and not count on Nick for anything. Meg tossed away the rest of her cookie and walked over to the sink. "I mean, it's been a hard enough night for him; don't make it worse."

"I'm not going to make it worse," Nick argued. He rubbed his forehead hard, as if he could iron

199

out all the confusion that was inside. "I want to make it better."

"It's kind of late for that," Meg came back immediately.

Nick stared at her. Meg sensed that she'd hurt him and was surprised that he still cared enough to be hurt. But it seemed to her that now *was* a little late for him to worry about Sean. Why was Celia the only one with the guts to stand up for Sean? Meg quickly ran cool water over her hands, no longer able to look at Nick.

"I didn't realize what was going on," Nick mumbled. "I didn't see it until it was too late."

Meg said nothing.

"When did this all happen?" Nick pleaded. "How was I supposed to know that Whitney was using Celia? I mean, I knew Whitney was after me — I'm not that dense — but how was I supposed to know that she was such a jerk? And why did Sean and Jay get into it like that? When did that start?"

Meg leaned against the counter. Where have you been all this time? she wanted to yell. Even I knew those jocks were gunning for Sean. And anybody who couldn't see that Whitney was a phony snob had to be wearing blinders. Meg felt the pull of tears as she thought about her own feelings. How could Nick have missed seeing that she was in love with him?

But it made her angry, too — white-hot angry. Sean had been humiliated, Allie hurt . . . Celia may have lost her best friend, and as far as Nick was concerned, she might as well have been a lump. Still, the thing that made her maddest was the way the whole group had let each other down. It was like a tent blowing away in a windstorm — nobody wanted to hold down the corners!

"Nick, I think maybe there's a lot of things you don't see."

"Like what? Meg, like what!"

Meg almost let go but she managed to pull back. It wasn't worth it. What good would it do if he knew about the way she really felt? It would only make things harder.

"Nothing," she finally managed, knowing she was about to cry. It made her furious that she couldn't deal with him anymore. She couldn't deal with him standing so close to her, his handsome face looking so weary, his hand held out to her as if he were begging for an answer. She had no answer to give him.

Nick ran a furious hand through his golden hair and looked at her again with pleading eyes. Meg pushed past him, just touching the fringe on his coat and the softness of his hand. She pushed on the door and walked out.

Allie and Celia left the quad and wandered across the parking lot. The moon was still high and bright. Kids were shrieking on the other side of campus and setting off what sounded like small firecrackers. The trees lining the side of the gym had been draped with toilet paper and someone had egged the windshield of Mr. Barnes' new Honda.

Allie and Celia stopped to inspect the gym teacher's car.

"Barnes'll love that," Allie laughed softly.

Celia looked tired but hopeful. She had Sean's sweater on over her long dress and her pale hair was pinned haphazardly atop her head. "Maybe we'd better not stand here. He might think we did it."

Allie led the way past the bike rack and toward the curb. They both hesitated when they noticed Sean's mountain bike still locked up. "I thought Sean left before us."

Celia looked behind her. "I guess not. I asked him if he wanted to walk home with me, but he said he wanted to ride home by himself."

"Do you think he's okay?"

"I think so. I'll call him tomorrow."

They continued walking in silence around the side of the school toward the flagpole and the main entrance. Allie headed for the pay phone and picked up the receiver.

Celia shyly stopped her. "Could you come over, Al? Maybe you could sleep at my house tonight."

"I'm sure my dad won't let me. I'm supposed to call him as soon as this is over."

Celia looked disappointed.

Allie thought for a moment, then put the phone back. "I guess I could walk with you to your house and call my dad from there."

Celia brightened. "Okay."

They walked silently, passing houses that were already decorated with black cats and witches on broomsticks. There were even a few jack-o'-lanterns lit in the windows and a parked car was covered with shaving cream.

When they reached Celia's house, they plopped

down on the front lawn. The moon looked huge and the street was quiet. For a while they sat there, both with their arms hugged around their knees and their feet exploring the overgrown grass.

"I'm sorry," Celia said finally in almost a whisper.

Allie rocked a little and her plastic charms clicked. "At least you finally told Whitney off."

"I should have done it a long time ago."

"Will it be weird having to be with her now for cheerleading?"

"Probably. It's been weird for a while. But not as weird as it was for us not to be talking."

They looked at one another, then down at the grass again.

"Cici. . . ." Allie hesitated. "Why did you tell Whitney my secret? How could you do that?"

"I don't know." Celia's voice got shaky. "I think I wanted to change. I wanted to be like them. I forgot the stuff that really matters."

"Like what?"

"Like my old friends. Like you being my best friend. Stuff like that." Two tears rolled down Celia's cheeks. "I really am sorry. Honest." She started to cry harder and lowered her cheek to her knees.

Allie rested her head on Celia's shoulder. "It's okay, Cici," she soothed, looking over at Sean's house across the street. "I guess this has been a hard time for all of us."

Celia lifted her head, and Allie extended her arms in a loving hug. Pretty soon they were both crying. Together.

*   *   *

The Haunted House was all closed up. Sean was insisting on biking home by himself. Allie and Celia had left a while ago. Meg walked across the deserted campus alone. She thought of calling her mom to come get her, but as she trudged along the edge of the quad she realized that she wanted to wander on her own. It wasn't that late, and her folks didn't expect her before eleven. She needed some time to think.

Meg passed the language labs and greenhouse and found herself heading over toward the playing fields. It was strange to see the corridors, usually crammed with students, now so dark and empty. All the classrooms were locked, but the walkways were lit and the gate to the parking lot was still wide open. Meg could hear a few voices and cars revving up and found herself looking away when she passed a couple kissing in the shadows outside the gym. She walked faster until she entered the stadium.

"Oh, Nick," she whispered as she reached the fence that surrounded the football field. She leaned her hands on the cold metal and rested her chin. She'd watched a few quarters of his games this season, but she couldn't bear the way he slammed his fist against his thigh when he did something wrong. And she couldn't bear the way Whitney constantly watched him, like a shark tracking an injured swimmer.

At least now he knew what Meg had known all along — that Whitney was a phony. Still, what did it matter? If it wasn't Whitney, it would be another girl just as flashy and as pretty — another to prove that Meg was dull and plain by comparison. Meg knew the answer wasn't for her to wear somebody else's dress, or to try and be the one who held everything together. But what was the answer?

Meg turned to leave, but as she did she saw someone sitting in the third row of the bleachers. Because there were no lights, she stared as he stood up, not sure if it was someone she knew or not.

"Hey, it's you again," Mark Coffield said easily. He was smiling down at her with his hands on his hips in a good-natured stance. In his letterman's sweater and khaki pants, he looked tall and wide-shouldered against the moonlit sky.

Meg wasn't sure what to do. The two exchanges she'd had with Mark so far had been total humiliation, and besides, why would one of the most popular boys in school — a senior — want to stick around and talk to her? Before she could go, he trotted down the benches, his arms bent in good running form, and joined her at the fence.

"Hi, Meg McCall." His smile was disarmingly open and friendly. He leaned on the fence, too, and the moonlight gleamed on his short hair and the sharp angle of his cheek.

Meg self-consciously laced her fingers in the fence and shook it once. "Hi."

Mark was staring out at the field. He rubbed his eyes, which made him seem momentarily troubled, boyish. When he caught her watching him, he gave an embarrassed shrug. Meg was so used to seeing him look confident and mature that his expression disarmed her . . . and made her feel a little less self-conscious.

"That Haunted House thing you did was great."

"Well, it was my class that did it really."

"Yeah, but you were in charge, right?"

Meg nodded.

The conversation ceased while they both stared out at the empty field as if an important game were being played there.

"How did you know that I was the one in charge?" Meg suddenly wondered. Even though a lot of upperclassmen had come to the Haunted House, she didn't think many paid attention to who did the work. Now that she thought about it, she wondered how Mark Coffield even knew her name.

Mark tapped his forehead. "I have ways." He bumped her with his elbow. "I probably shouldn't tell you this, but whenever new freshmen come, we check the girls out. The pretty ones, that is."

Meg looked over, stunned. She'd expected that boys like Mark would notice Celia or Whitney. But her? Meg McCall in her dad's suit jacket and faded jeans?

"You really noticed me?" Meg couldn't help asking.

He finally stopped gazing out over the playing field and faced her. The way he looked at her made her flush with embarrassment, and yet, she was smiling. He slowly shook his head and took a step back.

"I make it a policy to stay away from freshmen myself," he smiled, holding up his hands. "But if

I didn't. . . ." He whistled softly. "Besides, there's something special about you. Like the way you made the Haunted House happen. I don't know. You care." He stepped in again and pointed to the field. His arm was touching hers. Meg found it hard to think. "So, Meg McCall, do you think my dumb team will ever win a game?"

He said it with humor, but Meg knew losing hurt him almost as much as it did Nick. She also realized that he'd probably been sitting in those stands for a while, moping and praying for better luck in the few games left.

"I bet you win your next one," she said hopefully.

"You do?"

"I can feel it."

Before Meg could step back, Mark slid a gentle hand along the back of her neck, under her long hair. Impulsively he leaned forward and kissed her cheek. As he did, she could feel the slight rough stubble on his cheek and smell his licorishy aftershave. She almost lost her balance when he took his hand away. Her heart was leaping like a flying fish, and she felt breathless.

Mark looked like he was blushing, too. "I'd better get out of here before you make me change my policy." He stuck his hands in his pockets and backed up, still looking at her. "Somehow I think you may bring me luck, Meg McCall. I can feel that, too."

Meg watched him go. She was feeling like a helium balloon, as full as the moon overhead — and as bright and beautiful. She clung to the fence, her happiness building as she waited for Mark to trot away from the gym and into the parking lot. When at last she was sure that he was far, far away, she threw her head back, jumped up and down, and whooped as loudly as she could.

Meg finally left school and started for home, but Allie and Celia hadn't budged. They still sat together on Celia's front lawn. But the tears were gone. They'd been replaced by promises, more apologies, and big, bold Allie laughter.

Still, as much as Allie wanted to stay forever, sleep over, and talk endlessly with Celia, she knew she had to go home. The last thing she needed was to make her father worry again.

"I'd better go in and call home."

"I know." Celia looked inside. Her mother had just turned off the TV in the living room and was closing the curtains.

The girls started to go in and were brushing the grass from their skirts when Celia saw a lone bike rider appear around the corner. He rode slowly, pensively, and the streetlamps shone down on him like big flashlights.

"Sean!" Celia called. Allie waved, too, as Sean cycled closer. But he barely returned their greeting. He looked limp, almost frail as he pumped his legs wearily, and his bike wobbled toward them down the empty street.

Both girls started along the sidewalk to meet him. But before they reached him, an older model red Camaro rounded the intersection behind Sean. The car's headlights were blinding and it came around the corner so fast that both girls gasped.

The Camaro squealed to a halt, swinging over

to park on the wrong side of the street, right where Sean was dragging along. Sean stared for a split second, then he got off his bike, letting it clatter to the sidewalk, and took off in a run.

But he wasn't fast enough. The two doors of the Camaro flew open and three boys sprang out in pursuit. Celia and Allie — who stood frozen — recognized them immediately. Gus Baldwin. Bill Bloodgood. And Jay Creary. Before Sean could even cry out, the three football players had him wrestled to the ground. Then they picked him up and carried him sidelong, as if he were a manne-quin or a stack of lumber. And before Allie or Celia could get themselves to run over, Sean had been stuffed into the car and the doors were pounding shut.

The girls tore across the street as the Camaro made a vicious U-turn. Allie could barely see Sean in the back. Gus was practically sitting on him and the panic on his face turned her cold.

"What do you guys think you're doing?" Celia demanded. She tried to grab the window frame but the car swerved away.

Jay, who was driving, slowed briefly and smiled back at her. "You can come pick up your friend at the flagpole. That's where he'll be after he and I have a little talk."

Allie and Celia watched in horror. The last thing they saw was Sean's terrified face pleading to them through the back window as the Camaro sped away.

CHAPTER 19

Celia and Allie stared at Sean's mountain bike. It was lying on its side, half in the street, looking discarded, abandoned. A science manual and three comic books that had been in the basket were strewn along the sidewalk.

Allie picked up the bike as Celia collected the books.

"What should we do?" Allie asked in a desperate whisper. "Should we go tell his father?"

Celia clutched the books to her chest and looked over at Sean's house. Sean's father was proud and refused to let anything that he thought was wrong pass unpunished. He'd once chased a teenager ten blocks after the boy had stolen a bike bag from his shop. Celia could only think that it would be worse for Sean to have his father get involved in this.

"No," Celia said firmly. She walked fast, up

her own lawn and to her front door. Allie followed and leaned Sean's bike against the side of the house. The girls went inside.

"Let's call Nick," Celia decided. She could hear the shower running and her mother's off-key singing. Good. It was best if all the parents stayed clear of this one.

Celia dialed furiously, but the phone machine picked up. After leaving a message she slammed down the phone and handed it to Allie. "Stay here so he can call us back. I'm going to go see if Meg is home yet."

Allie nodded and Celia bolted out the door and started toward the pots and planters on Meg's porch. But before Celia reached the house she heard a soft whistle that alternated with a jolly hum. Turning back to the street she saw Meg.

It took a second before Celia could run toward her. Meg was walking along the very edge of the curb, her jacket tied around her waist, her arms out for balance or as if she were in some crazy ballet. Every few steps she'd take a twirl or a teeny leap, like she thought she was Gene Kelly or Jennifer Beals. Celia started for Meg and as she got closer, she saw a new, soft smile.

"Celia!" Meg cried out happily. She waved both hands over her head, and toppled off the curb into the street. She looked so happy and loose until Celia got closer, and Meg saw the alarm on Celia's face.

"They took Sean," Celia panted wildly.

Meg stiffened. "What?"

"Jay and two other guys. They put Sean in Jay's

car and said we could find him later at the flag-pole. I think they're going to beat him up or something."

Meg was already looking back toward Redwood High, ready to take off in a run.

Celia stopped her. "We need to have a guy with us. We need Nick. I tried to call but the machine is on. He should be home by now."

Meg had changed direction and was running toward Nick's. She called back, her hair flying behind her, "Keep trying. I'll run over there. Meet me later at the flagpole."

Celia closed her eyes as she watched Meg run and prayed that Sean would be all right.

"I should have stepped in and defended him, shouldn't I, Hugh? Even you would've done that."

Nick put an arm around Hughie and petted him on the soft part under his chin. Hughie looked up at him and cocked his head as if to say yes . . . even Hughie the dog would have stood up for Sean.

What an awful night, Nick thought as he sat on the grass in his front yard. He hadn't even gone inside the house. His folks were at a party, but he couldn't face going in and thinking about his father. At least his dad didn't know what a chicken he was.

How had he let things go so far? He'd seen Jay bully Sean the other day on the football field and not done a thing about it. He'd told himself that it didn't mean anything — jocks like Jay always did stuff like that. But inside he knew that part of him didn't want to be associated with

212

Sean because some people thought Sean was a nerd. Even his father made fun of Sean sometimes, and thought guys like Jay were manly and cool. Of course, his father was also the one that insisted he go out of his way to be nice to Whitney . . . and look where that led.

"How did things get so screwed up, Hugh?" Nick mumbled.

Nick suddenly felt something wet and warm slipping off his eyelid. He hadn't cried since the time he'd fallen out of the tree house and broken his arm when he was twelve. He remembered how he'd sat in the backseat of his dad's car on the way to the hospital. Meg and Sean had been with him. Nick had cried in front of them while Sean made jokes to try and cheer him up and Meg handed him Kleenex and chewing gum.

Nick missed his friends so much right now. He'd do anything if they could just start the year over. Simply push things back to the first day of school and make everything new. He wouldn't be so worried about impressing people or about football, and he'd stay closer to Sean and Meg and Celia and Allie. That's the first thing he'd do.

Suddenly, Hughie tensed and stood up. "Easy, boy," Nick said quietly, but Hughie didn't let up. A short, soft bark came out of his throat and his tail began thumping against the lawn.

Nick heard footsteps and looked up. Meg. She was running toward them and was passing under the streetlight. Her stride was as long and as pure as ever and her dark hair was shimmering under the lamp. Nick thought for a split second that she was the most beautiful girl he had ever seen.

"Nick! NICK!!"

Hughie bolted toward her, and Nick was up on his feet. He was so happy to see her, and without thinking, he ran toward her. Hughie was barking at his heels, but all Nick knew was that he had to take Meg in his arms. He had to feel her skin against his. She was running full speed, but when he opened his arms she fell against him as naturally as if they'd been standing still. For one long, wonderful moment, he held her while she panted and clung to him. He was holding her so tightly he could feel her heart pound. His own heart was beating just as hard. He felt his lips brush the side of her face, and she was just turning her mouth to meet his when she suddenly pulled back. That was when Nick realized that something was very wrong.

"We have to go to the flagpole at school . . . " Meg heaved, barely able to get the words out. Nick held her shoulders. He could feel how hot and damp she was through her T-shirt, and he wanted to wrap her up and protect her from the cool night air. ". . . It's Sean. Jay and two other guys took him over there."

Nick's anger came so strong and fast that he wanted to scream and cry all at once. He grabbed Meg's hands. "Are you okay now? Do you think you can run back?"

Meg swallowed hard and nodded.

"Let's go!"

Nick dropped her hands and they hit the street. Nick raced ahead and Meg ran right behind him.

They found Sean at the flagpole.

He was bound from the tops of his tennis shoes all the way up to his shoulders with heavy silver electrical tape. His face was pale in the moonlight, and he didn't say a word as they approached. But he looked at them with tears running down his cheeks.

"Sean. Oh, Sean, I'm so sorry."

Meg stood very close to him and touched his arm, which was taped tight to his thigh. Only the tips of his fingers were free. Nick got down on his knees and began slicing at the tape with his Swiss army knife. "Was it really Jay?" he demanded as he worked.

Sean shook his head back and forth. "Who do you think?"

The knife slowly moved up Sean's leg as Nick gingerly cut and peeled Sean away from the flagpole. Meg leaned her face against Sean's and felt his hot tears. "Those morons," Sean sobbed. "I'll kill them. I'll kill them!"

"It's okay," Nick tried to soothe. "You just leave it to me."

"Hey, you guys! Is Sean here. . . ?"

It was Celia and Allie coming from the other end of the school. They raced toward the flagpole. When they got there, both of them stopped and tried not to let Sean see how shocked and upset they were. At the same time, they both stepped in and tried to hug him.

"Watch it," Nick warned. "I've got to get this last part."

Allie apologized and stepped out of the way while Celia hooked her arm in Meg's. They stood there all together and waited for Nick to finish.

With the last cut, Sean stepped away from the pole. They pulled off the last pieces that stuck to his shirt and jeans and threw them away. Finally they all surrounded Sean, and held and hugged him to let him know that his ordeal was over.

"What are we going to do about this?" Meg said finally.

"That's right," Celia agreed. "Those jerks should — "

Just then a flashlight shone from across the schoolyard. Nick let out a breath and rolled his eyes. "Great. It's the security guy."

"What should we do?"

"I think," Allie spoke up, "that we should go somewhere and figure it out. But not my house — I'm sure I'm in enough trouble already."

Celia stood next to her. "Yeah, the last thing we need is parents right now." She looked off toward the security cop, who was walking closer.

"Where should we go?" Nick asked.

"I want to go to the tree house," Sean said in a low voice.

They all looked at each other, and then Meg put her arm around Sean, and the two of them began walking toward Nick's. The others fell in behind and they were on their way.

It was harder climbing at night, but at least the moon was high and bright so they could all see the branches. Nick's parents were still at their party, and he'd turned on the lights in the backyard to make the climb easier. Still, Meg got the feeling that they would have climbed even if it were pitch-black.

Nick was the one to make it to the top first, and when he did there was an audible groan. "What's wrong?" Meg called behind him.

"You'll see," Nick called back.

She did, too, as soon as she put her eyes over the top. A mess of damp rotting leaves had fallen and piled up over the floor, and the wood was dank and sour, almost as if the place were beginning to die. Nick was kicking furiously at the leaves and Meg had to put her hand on his arm to make him stop. It would have frightened Meg except that she understood how he felt. They'd come close to losing each other, and in some ways Nick had come closest of all.

"Let's just clear the floor off," Meg said calmly.

Nick didn't protest, and Meg cleared the rest of the leaves away herself. He secured the trapdoor so that Allie, Celia, and Sean would have an easier time coming up. In a minute they were there. Protectively, they helped Sean up. His face was streaked and dirty, but he was much calmer.

"Oh, no," Allie sighed as she crawled over with Celia.

"Look at all my stuff." Celia found one of her old thrift store vases. It was filled with dirty water, which she dumped over the side.

"Guess we should have done a better job storing everything," Sean said sadly as he picked up his old radio and shook some dead leaves off.

They all hesitated before sitting. But they had no choice, so they all settled down on the damp, clammy wood. A cold wind shook the top of the tree but only a few dark leaves were left to sail to the ground.

"I should have taken care of this place," Nick finally admitted. He looked around at all of them. "I guess I let a lot of things go lately."

"Me, too," whispered Celia.

There was a long silence, and Nick swatted the last of the wet leaves away. "I left you guys," he said in a sorry voice, "and I think I started to fall apart."

Celia reached over and put her arm across Nick's wide shoulders. He was folded up with his knees under his chin. Meg wanted to go over and hug him and let him know that it was all okay. But she didn't. She was still overwhelmed by the way he'd held her when she ran up to him. She didn't want to misinterpret anything or make things crazy and complicated again.

"Sean," Nick said again, "I'm really sorry. Those guys are jerks, and on Monday when I see them I'm going to. . . ."

"You're not going to do anything," Sean interrupted, sitting straight up.

Nick look surprised and his eyes, which had been staring at the tree trunk, now lifted to look at his friends. "What do you mean?"

"I've been waiting for you to make things okay for me. But I don't want that anymore. I don't want you to stand up for me. I don't want my parents to stand up for me. I can figure this stuff out for myself." Sean's voice dipped, but he pushed ahead anyway. "I don't have to be just like you, either. I have to do things my own way. And I will." Almost in tears again, he stopped speaking.

Nick nodded slowly, and Celia and Allie looked

218

at each other. Meg managed a smile. "I guess we all have to be ourselves. Sometimes that means we'll do stuff on our own and sometimes with each other. But what's most important is that we don't forget who we are."

"Or each other," Allie said.

"Or this place," Nick added, pointing around to the tree house.

Meg felt her spirits lifting. She looked up into the sky and saw the stars peeking through the leaves, and for the first time since she'd become a freshman she felt really whole again. She looked into her friends' faces and then placed her hands in the middle of their circle. Instantly they all knew what she was doing and their hands extended, too. Hand on hand, Meg nodded. "Then all of us proclaim that the tree house is officially reopened." Meg laughed.

"I'll keep it cleaned up," Nick volunteered. "Then if anybody wants to come here, it'll always be ready."

They all giggled, but nobody pulled their hands away; in fact, they held them together like that for what seemed a really long time. Finally they let go.

"Think this place will still hold us when we're seniors in college?" Sean wondered.

Celia reached over and punched him in the arm as Allie laughed and tousled his hair.

CHAPTER
20

The next morning, Allie woke early. Although there was a cold breeze, the sun was shining brightly in her window, but it wasn't the light or the chill that wakened her. It wasn't her strange dreams or her memories of the night before. It was the unusual mixture of voices coming from the other end of the house.

She was used to noise on Saturday mornings — her mom talking to Emily, Emily babbling in response, Fletcher's cartoon shows, her dad chatting with students on the phone. But this time there was another male voice coming from down the hall. It was higher, calmer, softer than her father's, and every once in a while she heard him laugh and her father laugh, too.

Allie sat up with a start. A buzz like an alarm clock had just gone from her bare toes to the collar of her long T-shirt. She knew who that voice sounded like.

"L.P."

It couldn't be. Still, just the thought of L.P. made Allie whip back her quilt and jump out of bed. In a rush to wash up, she ignored the pile of muddy clothes that she'd left on the floor the night before and hurried into the bathroom.

She hadn't even washed off her mascara before going to sleep last night, and this morning she looked like an owl. But she'd been so tired after she left the tree house, and of course, her father had been waiting up for her. When she'd explained about what had happened to Sean, he'd softened a little and told her they had lots to talk about in the morning.

Allie wasn't looking forward to that talk, but now that she kept hearing that L.P.-like voice, she quickly rubbed the makeup from under her eyes, brushed her teeth and hair, and slipped on a turquoise sweater and her bright pink jeans. Still sure that she was misleading herself, she crept down the hall and peered into the kitchen. When she did her eyes snapped open and her heart went into high gear.

"L.P.!" she gasped.

It *was* him. There he sat, between her father and Emily's high chair, sipping a cup of tea. When he saw her, he shot to his feet and looked a little embarrassed. His hair was wet and combed back, as if he'd made an effort to slick it down, and his camera was slung around his neck.

"Hi." L.P. gave her a very odd smile.

Her father was sitting back in his chair with his arms crossed. "Good morning, Al," he said in an ironic tone.

Allie blinked. The kitchen shades were up, and it was so bright she almost thought she was seeing things. But her vision did not alter. The more she stared the more clearly she saw L.P. He was wearing his dinosaur T-shirt and a green satin baseball jacket.

"Hi," Allie whispered as she lowered herself into a chair across from them. Her mom, still in her bathrobe, carrying Emily, came in for a cup of tea. She looked tired, as usual, but was smiling at Allie, giving her a don't-worry-I-softened-him-a-little look as she took Emily out into the living room.

Allie squirmed in the hard chair. "What are you doing here?" she finally managed to ask L.P.

L.P. sat down. He looked almost as uneasy as she, especially when her father leaned back even further and said, "L.P. came by here last night looking for you, Al." Mr. Simon rubbed his unshaven chin and looked at L.P. "L.P., would you tell Allie what you've been going through?"

L.P. looked like an unprepared student called on to give a hard answer. He fiddled with his camera, which sat on the table next to his teacup.

"Well" — L.P. cleared his throat — "I decided to come over here last night at the time when I knew the Haunted House was over" — he looked up at Allie for the briefest moment — "because I wanted to talk to you about something. But you weren't here and nobody knew where you were, and I waited here with your dad for almost an hour." He looked up again. "And I got really worried, so I stopped by this morning — I was on my way to take pictures in the park — just to

222

make sure that you were okay." He waited as Mr. Simon stared at Allie, then slugged back the last of his tea. "That's all."

Allie wasn't sure what to think. Was L.P. here to gang up with her dad against her? But when she looked at her father's round face, she didn't see the anger she'd expected to find there.

"Allie," Mr. Simon counseled, "I told L.P. what happened to Sean last night and how you had to help your friend. I know that it was important for you to help, and that you didn't know you were going to have to be out late. But if you'd called and told me what was going on, I wouldn't have worried." He smiled at L.P. "And L.P. wouldn't have worried, either."

Confused, Allie looked from her father to L.P. "But, Dad, you would have told me I couldn't stay and help Sean," Allie insisted, now embarrassed to be having this conversation in front of L.P., "or you would have come and got me, like you came and got me at the dance."

Mr. Simon leaned toward her. "Allie, I didn't know where you were the night of the dance, either. You'd told me you were with Celia and Meg and then I found out you weren't. For all I knew you were lying on a road somewhere."

"But you wouldn't let me go with L.P."

Mr. Simon held up his hands. "That's true, I didn't want you driving with L.P." Now, for some reason, L.P. was hiding his face. "Maybe I am too overprotective," her father went on. "L.P. seems like a sensible boy, and I certainly don't want to prevent you from spending time with him. But, Allie, we have to figure this out. Your mother and I have gone over this. We don't like grounding you, but we don't want to keep worrying about you, either. I know how you do things without thinking, how you're not careful." He let out a resolved sigh. "Let's make a deal. I won't punish you for last night, if you promise to always let us know where you're going and with whom. And not to lie." He stood up and stuck out his hand to shake.

Allie looked up at her father with new hope. He had an amused twinkle in his eye and his bald spot wasn't at all red. She knew that he would probably drive her crazy forever telling her to be careful, but at least, maybe, some progress was being made. "You really won't ground me again for last night?"

"Not if you promise."

Allie stuck out her hand. Her dad took it, but instead of shaking, he wrapped both his hands around hers in an affectionate embrace.

"It's a deal. Thanks, Dad."

Mr. Simon took his teacup over to the sink and turned back to her. "I have a feeling you two might want to talk, so I'm getting out of here." He pointed at Allie as if she were a failing student. "From now on, no more lying, and you're going to tell me exactly where you're going and with whom."

"Yes, professor," Allie teased.

Her dad came back over, softly touched her cheek, and then patted L.P.'s shoulder. "I've got papers to correct. I'll see you again . . . I hope," he said to L.P., then he left through the swinging door, and it was very quiet.

Neither Allie nor L.P. said anything for at least a minute. Allie drank her tea and L.P. examined his camera. They shifted and sighed as the kitchen clock ticked and the birds outside sang and whistled.

Finally L.P. got up and walked over to the sink. "He's not so bad," L.P. said. He turned to lay down his cup and saucer, but as he did he accidentally knocked over four plastic baby bottles that were drying on the counter. "Oh, no."

"It's okay," Allie said, scurrying over. She knelt and went for the bottles at the same time as L.P. She leaned in quickly, and then felt the top of her head whack against the top of L.P.'s. The room started to spin, and she grabbed her forehead. "OW!"

"I'm sorry," L.P. cried immediately. He touched her hair. "Are you okay?" He tried to scoop up the bottles again, but when he grabbed the fourth they all toppled onto the floor. "Darn."

Allie suddenly started to laugh. She couldn't help it. It was a huge, out-of-control Allie giggle, and soon L.P. was staring at her. At first he looked a little hurt, but then he started laughing, too.

"I'm not laughing at you," Allie panted. She was flapping her hands in that dopey way, but for some reason she didn't care.

"I know. It's all so ridiculous," L.P. chuckled.

They were both still kneeling on the kitchen floor. They were very close to each other and continued to laugh until L.P. looked into Allie's eyes and she felt her laughter stop. There was something about the way he looked at her, the sweetness, the openness of his gaze, that turned her wacky giggles into another feeling equally powerful, but much quieter and more contained.

L.P. took her hand. His palm was warm, and he slowly interlaced his fingers with hers. "I'm sorry I got you in all that trouble at the dance," L.P. blurted out. "That's what I came here to tell you last night. I should have told you way before this, but I was too ashamed."

"Ashamed of what? It wasn't your fault."

L.P. continued to hold her hand but looked away. "It *was* my fault. If I hadn't made such a big deal about driving, you never would have gotten in trouble."

"L.P., you're allowed to drive. Just because my dad is totally paranoid — "

Now L.P. squeezed her hand and raised his head. "I shouldn't have driven. I don't even have my license. I'm not sixteen yet. That's why my brother was so close by — I planted him there so there'd be somebody else in the car."

"You mean you — "

"I just wanted to impress you."

"But — " Allie started to laugh again. As she did her cheek fell onto the soft satin of L.P.'s shoulder. "No offense, but I did think you were a pretty bad driver."

Now L.P. was laughing again, too, and he playfully jabbed at her middle. "Now you tell me." He caught his breath. "Oh, Allie, can't we forget all that and start over? I thought we had a pretty good time together — after the beginning and before the end, that is."

Allie thought of the moldy leaves on the tree

house floor and how Meg and Nick had swept them away. She thought of Celia and how somehow she had swept that hurt away, too. Finally she looked up at L.P. and her insides lit up. Starting over was possible if you wanted it badly enough. "I can forget it," she said softly.

L.P. gazed at her, taking in her whole face until she blushed and felt almost giddy. He helped her stand and did not let go of her hands.

"Do you think you could come to the park with me today?"

Allie nodded. "I think so." She smiled. "There is one thing I'd better do first, though."

"What's that?"

"Tell my dad."

L.P. pulled her hands in closer until their noses were almost touching. Just when Allie thought she would faint right there on the kitchen floor, he slipped his hands around her waist and she put hers around his neck, and they helped to hold each other up with a round, gentle hug.

CHAPTER 21

It only took a week after the Halloween fund-raiser for the stadium lights to go up. And when they did, it seemed that every kid at Redwood was there for the first night game, even though their team had almost finished the season without a single win.

Allie and L.P. were huddled together, watching the game under a heavy blanket with Sean and Meg bundled up next to them. Redwood was playing Napa High and Celia and Nick were both down on the field, but every ten minutes, they would both look up to the others in the stands and grin or wave. Over their heads was a velvet black sky dotted with stars, and looking down on them like giant grasshoppers, those wonderful, awe-inspiring stadium lights!

"Meg, somebody's pointing at you again," Allie shivered and said.

Sean laughed. "You don't have to dress like

Madonna now. You're almost as famous already."

Meg pulled the cuffs of her heavy hand-knitted sweater down over her hands and flicked back the sides of her long hair to sit up proudly. Since halftime, when some man from the Rotary Club had dedicated the lights and asked Meg to take a bow, kids had been staring at her or coming up to offer congratulations. Meg felt like a celebrity.

But none of that really mattered. She was proud of herself, and of her class, and everybody was saying how great it was to finally watch a football game at night. It had been so long since she'd come to watch a game that she was just glad to be there.

The crowd suddenly leaped to its feet with a roar, and Meg and her friends rose, too. Mark Coffield had just thrown the ball. Nick was actually in the game and helped block a Napa player so that Jim Sale, the Redwood running back, was free to catch it. When Jim emerged from a pile of Redwood guys and was still holding the ball, Nick jumped up with excitement. The crowd exploded. It was the final quarter and they were tied 14–14. And they were near enough to the goal line to score.

But before play could begin again, a low moan went through the crowd. Meg wasn't sure what was going on. There was still a pile of guys a few feet from where Nick stood, and it looked like one in a red and blue Redwood uniform was taking a swing at a Napa player. The crowd was bobbing up and down, booing as about five Redwood guys crowded around the Redwood fighter and held him back. Finally the referee stepped in and booted him out of the game.

"Who was that jerk?" Sean asked, looking at his program.

"Number forty-two," said L.P.

"You won't believe this," Allie giggled, looking over Sean's shoulder, "but it's Jay Creary."

They all moaned until Meg shot up and pointed to the field. "Look at Celia!"

Sure enough, Celia was watching Jay get dragged off the field while cheering and executing ecstatic stag leaps.

"WAY TO GO REF!!!" Celia screamed, her pom-pom popping up into the sky. Whitney and Ann looked mortified and ran up to Celia, obviously informing her that she was cheering for the wrong side. Celia put a coy hand to her mouth, then blew a kiss up to Sean, and did another leap.

The ball went into play again, and this time, with only ten seconds to go, Mark Coffield ran with it himself. He raced and swerved past the opposing players.

"GO, MARK!!!"

"YES, COFFIELD!!!"

Everyone was screaming as Mark flew into the end zone, just as the final buzzer went off. Mark threw the ball into the air, raised his hands, and threw off his helmet.

The crowd went crazy. It was as if Redwood had just won the Super Bowl, instead of its first victory in a disastrous season. No one cared about that anymore. They'd waited a long time for a victory and they were going to enjoy it.

The crowd poured onto the field and Meg ran down, too. Players were leaping into girls' arms, and grabbing each other and jumping up and down. Meg felt overwhelmed in the midst of all these big, shoulder-padded hunks, and had started back toward the fence when Mark Coffield spotted her from a few yards away. His smile was as wide as the football field, and he looked incredibly handsome, although his hair was soaked with sweat and there was a bloody scratch along his cheek. He was grinning at Meg, and pumping his arm. And she was glad there were people all around to hold her up when she realized that he was heading over to her — otherwise she might have fallen into a puddle on the field.

"It was you, Meg McCall," Mark shouted as he pushed his way over. When he reached her he pulled her in with one arm and kissed the top of her head. His hand was hot and his shoulder pads banged her cheek, but Meg felt only pleasure. "I told you you'd bring me luck," he cried happily.

Meg smiled at Mark as he left her and was swept off with the other guys. She tried to get out of the crowd of players, but she was stuck. Everyone was too wild, too happy, and she was too woozy from Mark's attention. As she turned sideways and headed dreamily for the fence, someone grabbed her hand and stopped her. When she looked up to see who it was, she almost didn't recognize him. He was dappled with mud and grass and sweat and black paint. Still, there was no mistaking those piercing green eyes.

"Congratulations," Meg cried happily.

But Nick didn't look totally joyful. "Thanks." There was a tension on his face, a funny tightness. "I didn't know you knew Coffield."

Meg looked at him, puzzled. Then she realized that Nick must have been watching when Mark had put his arm around her and kissed the top of her head. "Oh, we've talked a few times," she answered.

Nick was looking back and forth between her and Mark, who was now being carried on the shoulders of the other players. He reached for Meg's hand again. "We're all going out for pizza after this, remember? All five of us, and L.P. Don't leave without me."

Meg almost laughed. "We won't."

Still staring at her, Nick jogged backward toward the gym. "I won't be long," he yelled.

Catching one more glimpse, Meg watched Nick go.

She thought about all the things she'd seen in those green eyes since they had all started high school — excitement, pride, confusion, anger, sadness. But she had just seen something new in Nick's expression. Jealousy — something she had learned about the first time she saw Nick and Whitney Hain together. Nick had that pinched, protective, what-are-you-doing-with-him? look in his eyes, and Meg wondered if maybe he did think of her as more than just a friend. Not sure whether to laugh or cry, she went back to where Allie, L.P., Celia, and Sean were waiting for her. When she joined them, she let loose with a cheer, threw her arms over her head, and leaped up.

"Yayyyyyy, REDWOOD!!"

When Meg hit the ground again, Sean was patting her shoulder, L.P. and Allie were right behind her, and Celia was on her other side. She looked back over toward the gym just as Nick was about to disappear inside. But as if he knew she was looking at him, he turned back and stared at her.

High school is going to be a very interesting four years, Meg thought to herself with a smile.

An interesting four years.

CLASS of '88

SOPHOMORE

"Meg McCall wants to be the first person to swim with all her clothes on in 1986," Jason teased.

"Jason!!!! Don't you dare!!" He was dipping her so far that her hair skimmed the top of the water. Meg was laughing and yelling and running out of breath all at the same time.

"That water looks so good."

"Put me down!!!" She beat against his strong back with her fists.

He inched closer to the edge. "Here we go."

Meg grabbed the collar of his rugby shirt and

held on tight. "If I go in, you're going in with me."

He started to spin around, and Meg closed her eyes, positive that the next thing she was going to feel was cold water and sharp chlorine. She prepared herself for the shock and clung to Jason, determined to drag him in, too. Then she felt him lose his balance, and they both began to tumble, leg over leg, arm over middle onto something much harder than water, something springy, fragrant, and only slightly damp. She opened her eyes to see that Jason had spun away from the pool and the concrete, and they were spilled on a soft section of thick, lush grass. It was cold and the dew was already soaking through the back of her blouse, but Jason had toppled down next to her and he was very warm.

She rolled onto her back and Jason moved in close, leaning above her on one elbow. He made a move to wrestle her, but she blocked him and started laughing hard. "Oh, no, you don't."

He held up one hand as if to prove that he was no longer on the attack, then he gazed into her face. His brown eyes lost their usual bright alertness and instead looked a little sleepy. Meg started to giggle again.

"What's so funny?" Jason demanded, pretending to be insulted.

"You!" Meg laughed. "You just make me laugh." She let herself go, sighing and laughing. Jason made her feel like a little kid.

He sat up and grabbed her arm, playfully pulling it behind her back. "Nobody laughs at Jason Sandy," he said in a voice halfway between Marlon Brando and Humphrey Bogart.

Meg was about to ask him who he was trying to imitate when the party inside exploded. Horns began tooting, people were screaming. Meg and Jason sat up together on the lawn.

"It's 1986," Meg said.

Jason was looking at her with those sleepy eyes again. "You know the first thing I want to do this year?"

"What?"

He paused. "Kiss you."

He put a hand to her chin and closed his eyes. At first Meg still wanted to giggle. Then his soft mouth met hers and they fell back on the grass and she felt so warm and breathless that giggling was the last thing she wanted to do.

Inside, on the sun porch, Kristin McGraw was kissing Nick's cheek, and Hilary Tate was grabbing him so tightly around the neck that he thought he might choke.

"Happy New Year!!!" Hilary yelled, right in Nick's ear.